Billy Ray's Forty Days

Also by Frank Roderus
in Large Print:

Charlie and the Sir
J. A. Whitford and the
    Great California Gold Hunt

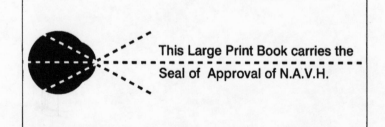

Billy Ray's Forty Days

Frank Roderus

Thorndike Press • Waterville, Maine

Published in 2004 by arrangement with Frank Roderus.

Thorndike Press® Large Print Christian Fiction.

The tree indicium is a trademark of Thorndike Press.

The text of this Large Print edition is unabridged.
Other aspects of the book may vary from the original edition.

Set in 16 pt. Plantin by Al Chase.

Printed in the United States on permanent paper.

Library of Congress Cataloging-in-Publication Data

Roderus, Frank, 1942–
    Billy Ray's forty days / Frank Roderus.
        p. cm.
    ISBN 0-7862-6450-0 (lg. print : hc : alk. paper)
    1. Clergy — Fiction.   I. Title.
PS3568.O346B54 2004
    813′.54—dc22   2004051713

For Julie Marie Roderus

As the Founder/CEO of NAVH, the only national health agency solely devoted to those who, although not totally blind, have an eye disease which could lead to serious visual impairment, I am pleased to recognize Thorndike Press* as one of the leading publishers in the large print field.

Founded in 1954 in San Francisco to prepare large print textbooks for partially seeing children, NAVH became the pioneer and standard setting agency in the preparation of large type.

Today, those publishers who meet our standards carry the prestigious "Seal of Approval" indicating high quality large print. We are delighted that Thorndike Press is one of the publishers whose titles meet these standards. We are also pleased to recognize the significant contribution Thorndike Press is making in this important and growing field.

Lorraine H. Marchi, L.H.D.
Founder/CEO
NAVH

* Thorndike Press encompasses the following imprints: Thorndike, Wheeler, Walker and Large Print Press.

1

"Is this, uh, it?"

The stagecoach driver looked at him and chuckled. "Not much, huh? You were expecting Kansas City, maybe?"

Billy Ray Halstad shrugged. And sighed. He wasn't entirely sure what he'd expected of Purgatory City. But truth to tell, this wasn't exactly it.

Seen from a distance of several miles Purgatory City looked to be little more than a collection of gray, weathered shacks clustered along a line of dusty green foliage that marked a river or stream bed in this sere, ocher and brown country.

The river would be the Purgatory. Or the Picketwire. Or whatever else you wanted to call it. The folks who'd called him here had gone to great lengths to explain in their letters that the name of the river had nothing to do with hell or damnation or purgatory itself.

Somewhere back along the string of time the river'd been called by the old-time

Spanish the River of Lost Souls. And then some Frenchman had changed that to the Purgatoire. And then some cowboys took to calling it the Picketwire in a corruption of that name. And modern maps put it down as the Purgatory. And the town took its name from that. More or less.

Standing up here on the bluff overlooking the valley while the coach driver rested his team from that last sharp incline, Billy Ray wasn't so sure all those name-naming folks hadn't got it right all along and that it was purgatory he was looking at.

The country was that dry and burnt-looking, all reds and browns and yellows, even the green along the water flow looking dried out and forlorn.

Billy Ray glanced wistfully back toward the west. But all he could see back that way now were brown, barren plains and brown, lumpy mesas. There wasn't a hint on the horizon of the tall, cool mountains that had been his home for so long.

This time of year the Rockies were snowcapped and majestic, and a man always . . . at least Billy Ray always . . . felt close to God when he was up there.

Down here . . . he shivered . . . down here he felt nearer to purgatory than he did to Purgatory City.

He sighed again.

There wasn't anything for him back in those mountains now.

Blue Gorge was gone. Closed up tight and by now weathering and decaying, with only the hawks and the mice left to care that there'd been a town there once where miners caroused and babies were born, and now and then a soul was saved.

The veins of gold and silver played out, and one by one the mines closed down, and now there wasn't hardly anything left at all to show that once there'd been such a place as Blue Gorge.

And now Billy Ray's future lay down there in Purgatory City whether he liked it or not, because that was where they said they needed him, and that was where he would go.

"You all right, Reverend?"

"I'm fine, thank you."

"Best get back in then, Reverend. I think we can start down now." The sweat was drying on the horses' broad shoulders, and if the driver let them cool too much more they would start to stiffen and get tight, and they might get themselves in trouble on the steep downhill grades to come.

Billy Ray crawled back inside the Studebaker coach that had been bouncing him like a pea in a confidence man's shell for the past day and a half. He pulled the door shut behind him and made sure the latch was securely set. "All right, John."

"Hang onta your hat, Reverend." John released the brake and shook his lines, and the coach rocked forward and began to angle down.

"You sure this is what you had in mind, Lord?" Billy Ray asked inside the privacy of the coach.

The Lord didn't offer any last-minute reprieve from Purgatory City.

2

There wasn't any regular stage station in Purgatory City, but the place did seem larger close up than it had from the top of the hill to the north.

There was one wide, crooked area of bare, beaten earth that could pass for a main street. That had lines of false storefronts lining it with their backs to the Purgatory River and a somewhat thinner line of buildings facing them across the dirt at a distance of forty or fifty yards. The main-street buildings were not divided into formal blocks but seemed to have been plunked down wherever their owners pleased, with narrow alleys and wider, streetlike openings separating them by whim rather than design.

All around this gray, weathered business district there were randomly scattered houses and shacks and cabins laid out with no particular plan or order, so that there seemed to be no side or cross-streets in the town.

Billy Ray got the impression that Purgatory City had grown like a patch of weeds rather than been planned like a garden.

What it was now, of course, was his vineyard to tend.

The coach rolled past the first of the buildings and on into town, and he could feel his stomach turn sour and begin to churn as the uncertainty of it all struck him.

What if they didn't like him here? What if he failed them? What if *he* didn't like *them?*

What if . . . ?

He had been assailed by doubts for the past month and a half, and a month and a half of worrying about it had not removed a single one of those fears. Not a one.

And seeing Purgatory City did nothing to remove them either.

He sat back against the seat of the Studebaker and fought a desire to just stay on the darn coach. To not announce his presence and just keep going.

Except, whether Billy Ray liked it or not, the coach would not be going on.

From here it would just turn around and go back to Trinidad.

John had explained it to him on the way here. Purgatory City was the end of the line. The express company wouldn't even have agreed to provide service out this far except

12

mail delivery to and from Purgatory City was a necessary part of a bid for a mail contract the company wanted.

Billy Ray stared out the coach window at the unfamiliar buildings and the few unknown faces in sight.

Purgatory City was the end of the line, all right.

But in just how many ways?

Billy Ray's stomach knotted tighter, and he could feel sweat gather under his arms. The sweat had absolutely nothing to do with the day's heat.

He should have . . . he didn't know . . . gone to another mining camp? Gone back to operating a hoist? It was honest work. There wasn't anything wrong with honest labor.

At home in Blue Gorge he'd become comfortable with his preaching.

But that was with people he knew. People he'd worked with. People who knew him.

Here . . .

The coach rocked to a halt on its leather-sprung suspension, and John called down, "All out for Purgatory City," making a joke of it, as Billy Ray was the only passenger he had on the long run from Trinidad.

"Time to get out, Reverend."

"Thank you, John."

13

They were stopped in front of a rickety, one-story log structure with a poorly constructed two-story false front attached to the street side of it. A sign over the door read *Walker Ayres, Mercantile.*

Billy Ray Halstad girded his figurative loins and stepped down onto the dirt main street of his new home.

3

He hadn't expected a brass band. But someone to say hello and show him where the manse was would have been nice.

Billy Ray collected his suitcase from the luggage boot on the back of the tall Studebaker, while John was busy unloading a mail sack from the driving box and carrying it inside the store.

The mail pouch was regulation stuff, heavy canvas and thick leather and impressive-looking padlocks. Judging from the way it flopped loose in John's hand, though, there couldn't have been more than a few thin letters in it. No wonder the stagecoach line was unenthusiastic about having to keep Purgatory City on their route; even letters didn't travel here often.

Billy Ray looked down at the suitcase dangling from his hand and made a wry face. Then grinned. He wasn't traveling a whole lot heavier than that mail pouch, actually. A couple spare shirts, extra underwear, one spare pair of trousers slightly threadbare, shaving kit with razor, strop, brush, soap and comb. One winter coat with muffler. And two Bibles. That was the extent of what he owned after thirty-two years in this particular life.

Oh, yes. He'd forgotten his socks. He had an extra pair of socks. He should have remembered those in his inventory.

And he had a dollar fifty-three cents cash money in his right-hand pants pocket and a handkerchief in the left-hand pocket.

If the good people of Purgatory City hadn't sent him the coach ticket he wouldn't have had enough money to get here after four years of trying his best to spread the Good News.

Now . . . here . . . Billy Ray shivered as a chill crawled up and down his spine.

That was pure coincidence, of course. He *knew* that. Still . . .

He set the battered suitcase — it was a cast-off thing that someone had left behind when they abandoned Blue Gorge; Billy Ray had plucked it off one of the many trash dumps that had appeared along the street in those last days, thinking it would be better than packing in a burlap bag for the journey south and east — on the weathered boards of the sidewalk and stepped up onto the porch just as John was coming back outside with another limp mailbag in his hand.

"Thank you for all your kindness on the trip, John," Billy Ray told him.

The coach driver stopped and blinked, as if surprised by the thanks. "Why, sure, Rev'rend. You're welcome. My pleasure."

"Will you be staying over tonight?" Billy Ray was thinking that if John would be here perhaps they might have supper together or something like that. Just so he could count on seeing a friendly face his first night in Purgatory City.

"Oh, I never do that, Reverend. Just in an' back out again. No team relay here, so I always go back to the Parker place. You remember them? Where we had breakfast? 'Course you do. Anyhow, I always go back there an' sleep on the backhaul. Sure would be nice could we arrange for a team change here." He sighed, making that simple desire seem an impossibility. It was no wonder he wished for a layover here, though. The run back to the Parker ranch would keep him on the road until nearly midnight, Billy Ray guessed. "Well, Rev'rend, I better get on. It was nice meetin' you."

John acted like he didn't know whether he

should tip his hat or shake hands. Billy Ray solved the dilemma for him by offering a hand.

" 'Bye, Reverend."

" 'Bye, John."

The level of Billy Ray's disappointment seeing John crawl back onto the Studebaker and drive away was unpleasantly high.

Part of that, he suspected, was knowing that the coach would not return to Purgatory City for another full week.

This was Wednesday. The coach from Trinidad left there every Tuesday and returned each Thursday. From one Wednesday to the next, Purgatory City was as good as isolated from the rest of the world, unless a man had his own transportation.

Billy Ray felt that shiver chase its tail along his spine again.

He left the suitcase unattended on the sidewalk — there was no one around to bother anything even if there was anything in the bag worth bothering; and come to think of it, why was everything so quiet and closed-up on the day when the mail and the one and only coach rolled in — and went inside the store.

If he was going to be here — and he was sure going to be here, at least for a while —

he might just as well start meeting some of the folks he would be ministering to in the days or months or years to come.

4

"Mr. Ayres?"

The man Billy Ray took to be Walker Ayres was behind the cluttered counter of the store. He was large and rumpled and several days unshaven, perched on a tall stool near his cash box. He wore a coat and high-buttoned but collarless shirt with no tie. Ayres appeared to be in his middle years, an age that suggested he was almost certainly the proprietor of the store and not an employee.

The man was busy opening the mail pouch John had brought inside moments earlier. He hadn't looked up when Billy Ray came in. Now he glanced toward the new-comer with a frown, and made a critical head-to-toe inspection of this intruder inside the otherwise empty store.

"I don't need no new suppliers whatever 'tis you're peddling. You best see can you catch that stage quick 'fore it strands you till next week." He looked back down at the mail pouch. Although there certainly was not so much in there that it could have held anyone's attention very long. He pulled out a slim handful of letters and shuffled through them, pocketed one and tossed the others casually into a wooden box on a shelf behind him.

"You would be Mr. Ayres?" Billy Ray persisted.

The man grunted. "Said that a'ready, didn't I?"

In fact he had not, but it hardly seemed a point worth arguing over. "Sorry," Billy Ray said with an apologetic smile. He approached the counter and offered his hand, which Ayres pretended not to see.

Billy Ray grinned and left his hand extended, right where it was, not pulling back a quarter of a darn inch.

"I am Billy Ray Halstad, Mr. Ayres. The Reverend Halstad? Your new preacher? I was called here to take over the church?"

Ayres looked up again. His frown deepened and once more he grunted. Now it was impossible for him to pretend that he didn't see Billy Ray's offer of a handshake.

Walker Ayres stared first into Billy Ray's eyes. Then down at the extended hand. Then back into Billy Ray's eyes. His own eyes shifted nervously for a moment. He hesitated. Then cleared his throat and turned his head away to spit in the general direction of a largish tin can that was serving as a cuspidor.

"I see," Billy Ray said. Although he did not. He pulled his hand back and jammed it down into a pocket.

Ayres blinked but said nothing. He was very carefully looking anywhere but at Billy Ray now. He did not act ashamed, exactly . . . but he looked like he felt almost as nervous now as Billy Ray most certainly did.

Ayres cleared his throat again.

"Is there something you want to tell me, Mr. Ayres?"

"Nope." Ayres had taken the letter from his pocket and was fiddling with it, idly turning it over and over in his hands, which Billy Ray noticed now were large and lumpy with calluses, work-hardened hands that Ayres had not gotten by sitting behind a store counter with a cash box and a mail pouch.

"Very well. Thank you very much, Mr. Ayres." Billy Ray tipped his hat and gave the storekeeper a smile that Ayres did not see, thanks to a sudden preoccupation with his own fingernails.

Billy Ray turned toward the front door.

"Halstad?"

"Yes, Mr. Ayres?" He stopped.

"East end o' town. That, uh, that's what you want."

"Thank you, Mr. Ayres. Thank you kindly."

Billy Ray gave Walker Ayres a wave that was not acknowledged. He went outside to collect his bag and carry it along the street in a direction that was more or less easterly.

5

The church wasn't, perhaps, what Billy Ray had expected.

It wasn't, in fact, very much.

And that was to put a charitable face on things.

He found it at the eastern edge of Purgatory City, the easternmost structure of the ragtag collection of buildings that made up the town.

The sanctuary was identifiable because someone had thoughtfully used some two-by-six timbers to construct a ragged, rugged, warping cross and nail it to the roof peak on the front of the place.

The cross was perhaps the most solidly constructed portion of the entire building, Billy Ray saw, as he hiked slowly and with no small degree of nervousness toward "his" new church.

Actually, of course, the building was His, not his. Not Billy Ray's. But the Reverend Billy Ray Halstad was not entirely sure He would want to claim the place. Or that he would either.

It would require, Billy Ray suspected, an act of considerable faith just to walk inside the church building and expose oneself to the dangers of the sagging roof and slumping walls.

The closer to it he came the more he had to work at suppressing frowns and shudders.

The walls had been made of slender aspen logs that over the years had dried and warped, until butt and tip ends here and there were sprung entirely away from the crudely notched joints at the corners.

The roof was made of light aspen saplings that were also warped now. Originally the roof had been covered with split shingles of . . . pine? Possibly . . . but now only enough shingles remained in place to show that once there had been a roof.

The floor — bare, beaten earth — was dappled with more light than shadow, as the sunshine slanted in through the gaps where shingles should have been.

Billy Ray could see all this quite well without going inside, because there was no door hung on the logwork frame at the front of the place.

Which was probably just as well, he reflected, because one good, angry slam of a front door could bring the whole thing tumbling down on itself.

Before stepping foot inside the sanctuary he grimaced and hunched his shoulders, and prudently set his suitcase on the ground outdoors.

In case he had to make a lifesaving leap to safety he did not want to be encumbered by baggage.

From the doorway he could see — actually, he thought, he could almost as easily have peered through the walls; there was more than enough room to see through the gaps between the crooked logs — that the place was furnished with six split-log benches, each long enough to support four or five worshipers; they were arranged three on either side of the open floor, leaving an aisle of sorts in the middle.

At the front there was no raised dais or pulpit, although there again someone had built and hung a crude cross as a reminder that this was, after all, a church building.

Billy Ray lifted his cloth cap and ran a hand over his scalp, then, cap in hand, stepped inside the church at Purgatory City.

"I suppose it's too late for You to turn

that stagecoach around and send it back here," he said aloud.

After a moment he added, "I didn't think so."

6

He probably should have been spending his time praying. Probably. At the moment he just plain didn't feel like it. So he worked instead.

The town dump of Purgatory City was depressingly close to the church building. Which was a left-handed advantage of sorts, since the dump supplied Billy Ray with several handy articles.

A leaky bucket that someone had thrown away worked well enough to carry water to the church from the nearby Purgatory River. If he started from the riverbank with a full bucket, he still had two thirds of a bucket left by the time he reached the church. And a wet pants leg too, of course, but he could get along with that.

He pulled the benches out into the sunshine and began flooding the dirt floor with river water. Thoroughly wetted and then allowed to dry, the earth would take on a hard surface crust that could be tamped firm and later swept. Given enough time, enough wettings and enough tamping and sweeping afterward, the dirt would become almost a real floor.

He labored from the church to the river and back again with the bucket, until his trousers were soaked and his hands hurt from the bail of the bucket digging into his palms with the weight of the water.

It was tempting to start out with lighter loads and fill the bucket only partway, but what with the leakage along the way that would have meant arriving at the sanctuary with so little water left that the trip would not be worthwhile making to begin with.

So he kept doggedly on, two thirds of a bucket at a time until the entire floor was thoroughly wet, if not exactly flooded.

While the now muddy floor dried, Billy Ray sat on one of the split-log pews in front of the church and made himself a broom for later use. A length of dead sapling gathered along the river, some pine boughs and some twists of scrap wire from the dump were enough to let him make a broom. It wouldn't be pretty but it would work well enough for his purposes.

He was sitting in the shade, smoothing out pieces of discarded wire, when he heard the rattling approach of a light wagon from downriver. The wagon held two men and a woman and was moving in a hurry.

The driver was headed into town, but a shout and a pointing finger — directed at the church with Billy Ray sitting on a pew outside it — made the driver swerve violently off the road in Billy Ray's direction.

The wagon rocked to a halt a few feet in front of Billy Ray. Its occupants were breathless and distressed even though it was the unmatched team of small mules that had been doing all the work.

"Reverend Halstad?"

"Yes, sir." Billy Ray laid his wire aside and stood.

"Sorry we wasn't there to meet you off the coach. Started out in plenty o' time but had an axle break. Had to go borry this rig off Andrews, you see, an' what with walking to his place an' going back to fetch Mother an' then . . . well anyway, I'm sorry."

Billy Ray chuckled and brushed his hands off as the folks climbed down off the wagon box.

He hadn't even met these people yet and already he was feeling better about his situation here. Much better.

It looked like he had a congregation after all.

7

The older of the two men was Elizander Pieck, the gentleman who had handled the correspondence that brought Billy Ray here. The couple were Adler and Norma Smits. All three folk of his new congregation were dressed poorly, the men in bib overalls and Mrs. Smits in a plain dress with a wilting wildflower pinned to it in an attempt to spruce up for the occasion.

"Ad is the other deacon," Pieck explained after the introductions were made and the mules had been tied to a hitch weight. "You recall I wrote you about him? Ad's been doing the preaching up till now for us."

Pieck was smiling, but Ad Smits was not. Billy Ray couldn't help wondering if the farmer deacon felt he should have been given the pulpit — such as it was — of the Purgatory City church, instead of calling in a stranger for the task.

"It's a great pleasure to meet all of you. I can't tell you how much I've been looking forward to getting here," Billy Ray said, even though he knew he wasn't supposed to lie.

Eli Pieck returned more of the same and managed to sound like he meant it. Ad Smits said very little. And Mrs. Smits said nothing at all.

"Will it be possible for me to meet the other, um, members of the congregation soon? Or must I wait until Sunday?" Billy Ray asked.

"On the Sabbath," Smits said. "We all cain't afford to waste time, Halstad. Bad enough losin' t'day's work. Labor for the six days, give the seventh t' the Lord. That is the way 'tis written; that is the way 'tis done." His voice was sonorous and sorrowful. Billy Ray thought he could detect a half-hidden note of accusation in it too, as if the new preacher had just asked everyone in the community to neglect their duties in favor of a gala on his behalf, or something.

Billy Ray smiled and stuffed his hands into his pockets. "That gives me something to look forward to for the next few days then, doesn't it?"

Smits grunted.

"You'll be wanting to see your new quarters," Pieck injected.

"Indeed I would, Mr. Pieck."

"Eli. Please call me Eli, Reverend."

"And I'm Billy Ray," he said with a smile and a nod. He glanced at Smits. "Or whatever."

Smits was frowning.

"This way, Reverend. I mean, Billy Ray." Pieck seemed eager and happy.

"You show 'im, Eli. The missus and me'll wait here with the team."

Pieck nodded and set off at a heavy, ponderous gait that hinted of rheumatism or old injuries, one leg not quite keeping up with the other as he walked.

The way led around behind the rickety church, past the sun-scorched dump toward a weathered door set into a hillside. Billy Ray had noticed the door before, during his trash-picking for the bucket and wire, and took it to be a root cellar.

As it turned out, the "root cellar" was an old dugout. A habitation — more or less — dug out of a south-facing hillside, then roofed over with poles and sod, and faced with timber and a door.

Billy Ray had heard about dugout houses, of course, and had seen a few in passing, but he had never set foot inside one before.

Most of his adult years had been spent in mountain mining communities, and he honestly had not thought of himself as being particularly citified. Or inexperienced. Before he found the Truth he'd had his moments as a wastrel and a hellion. But all his previous experience had been inside buildings or tunnels. And he'd learned to hate and fear mine tunnels.

He looked at the small dugout and shuddered.

The mostly underground cabin — which was what it was, essentially — reminded him much too much of a short mining adit.

The main difference was that instead of hundreds or thousands of feet of solid rock over his head, in the dugout he would have overhead a few flimsy, aging aspen poles and several feet of dried-out sod.

Billy Ray had seen one mine cave-in. He didn't want to experience a miniature version of that here. There was enough sod on the roof to crush and suffocate a man if it all came tumbling down on top of him.

Eli Pieck was still smiling. He showed off the dugout with pride.

"She's not new, but she's sound," he was saying. "Been here a long time, this'un has. I know the fella that dug her. Used to live in her when he first come to this country. He gave her to us so's you would have a place of your own close by the church. Done it in writing so there couldn't be no quarrel about the rights."

Pieck pulled the door open. It was hung on brand-new chunks of thick leather.

"You can see we fixed her up some. Cleared out the trash was in her an' nailed on new hinges. Ira Jolly had a steel stove that he donated for you. Andrews built the bunk and stools . . ."

Whoever this Andrews was, Billy Ray hoped he was a better craftsman than whoever had built the church and the pews.

"Leo Tyson and his boys made you the table an' a writing desk. An' we all pitched in with a little o' this and a little o' that for lamps an' plates and such. You oughta be real comfortable here, Reverend." He grinned. "I mean, Billy Ray." The grin became a chuckle. "You'll forgive me, I hope. Gonna take some time to get used to calling you by name. Ad, he takes the Lord serious. Likes to be called Deacon on Sundays though it's Ad the rest of the week. Hope you don't mind."

"I don't mind," Billy Ray said automatically. He was feeling somewhat distracted actually, and eyed the roof with some trepidation before trusting himself to step inside the dugout house.

Standing in the doorway, he could see

that it wasn't really as bad as he had feared.

From the outside the dugout looked like nothing more than a hole in the ground. But inside it seemed almost like a house, except, of course, for the lack of windows.

The floor was packed and swept, and actually in much better shape than the church floor, perhaps because the interior of the dugout had been better protected from weather through the years. And the walls were lined with a facing of piled stone so that the impression, except for the pole-and-sod roof, was of a stone house and not an underground one.

There was a cot with a grass-stuffed ticking mattress tucked into a back corner on the right. The middle of the single room was dominated by a sturdy table, with four stools arranged around it. There was a sheet-metal stove centered against the back wall with pipe sections extending up through the roof. Another stool and low table — apparently the writing desk Pieck had mentioned — were set against the left wall. Above them were several shelves mounted into the stones of the wall. One of the shelves held a shiny new lamp. And there was another lamp sitting on the table.

Crates had been piled together to fashion doorless cabinetry close to the stove, and these held a small assortment of dishes and cutlery and old pots.

There was a full woodbox next to the stove, and a new box of sulphur-tipped matches just where Billy Ray would have chosen to put them himself.

"It looks like everyone has pitched in and contributed something here," Billy Ray said. "I'll not be able to thank them myself until services on Sunday, Eli. I hope, well, any of the folks that you see in the meantime . . ."

Pieck grinned and nodded. "I'll tell them, Reverend. Billy Ray, that is. I'll surely tell them."

Billy Ray felt better now than he had since he first rolled into sight of Purgatory City from the distant hilltop.

"Oh, yes. Before I forget," Pieck said. "There's a well in the yard over there," he pointed, "but the sides fell in a spell back. Got to get your water from the town well." He pointed again. The town was a good three hundred yards away from the dugout, between the hillside of Billy Ray's new home and the Purgatory River, and lying a little west of the dugout. Immediately south of the dugout was the dump, while east of that was the church building.

From the front door of his new home Billy

Ray would have a good overview of the river, the town and everything that went on.

But nowhere could he see mountains or high snowfields.

It occurred to him with considerable surprise that what he was here was homesick.

"Best be getting back to Ad and his missus," Eli suggested. "Ad, he'll be getting nervous bein' away from his labors so long."

Pieck and Billy Ray walked back to the wagon and the waiting Smitses, and Billy Ray said all the expected thank-yous and glad-to-be-heres and see-you-Sundays, shook hands with the gentlemen and doffed his cap to Mrs. Smits.

It was only after the other three had climbed back onto the wagon and rumbled away toward the east — not even stopping at any of the town stores although they were right there, practically beside them on a weekday afternoon — that Billy Ray realized he should have offered to lead prayer with the new congregation members before they drove off.

But it was too late.

He mumbled an apology of sorts to himself or to the Boss, he wasn't sure which, picked up his suitcase and trudged back toward the dugout that was to be his home for the foreseeable future.

8

There were kitchen utensils in the dugout, but nothing to cook with them. Wood in the box, but no purpose to starting a fire. Billy Ray fingered the coins in his pocket and decided that just this once he could buy a meal. Just for this first night.

From here on, of course, he would have to be careful. The congregation had agreed to pay him a regular salary, saying in one of Brother Eli Pieck's letters that it wouldn't be possible for him to get a regular job in Purgatory City — although there hadn't been any explanation about why that was supposed to be so — so they would pay him twelve dollars a month if Billy Ray would come take over the pulpit. The amount should be entirely adequate if not exactly generous.

But tonight, just this one time, he would walk into town and buy a regular meal.

After the jolting and lurching of the stagecoach and the catch-as-catch-can meals at the infrequent stage stops, Billy Ray simply did not feel up to buying foodstuffs and then cooking for himself.

Actually, he didn't know whether he should smile or shudder at the thought of cooking for himself in the future. It wasn't something he'd ever had to do before.

In the mines there had always been boarding houses that prepared meals for the men. And later, when he was preaching in Blue Gorge and working the rest of the time, well, he'd not had much, but enough that he could buy a meal when he was hungry. He really never had learned to cook. Apparently he was going to have to take it up now.

He deposited his things in the dugout and wandered into town. It was only a five-minute walk, and one he rather expected to get used to in the near future.

Billy Ray had no trouble at all deciding where to eat. There was only one place that offered meals. And it did not depend solely on a restaurant trade for its survival; the front portion of the establishment held shelving and counters where the proprietor also sold notions, stationers supplies, patent medicines and the like. Most of the wares on display there had a dusty, sun-faded look that hinted they had been in place for a very long time.

It was early for the supper trade, and the only other customers seated in the dining portion of the place were a pair of elderly men wearing the high-heeled boots and broad-brimmed hats of cattlemen, unlike the farmers who had come to the church to welcome the new preacher.

Billy Ray greeted the men as he chose a seat, and was given a matched pair of scowls in return.

He smiled at them anyway. "Evening, gentlemen. I'm Billy Ray Halstad. The new preacher."

The two old men ostentatiously turned their chairs so their backs were toward him, and leaned low over their coffee cups, dropping their voices to whispers that he could not overhear.

He decided he likely shouldn't count on seeing either of the gentlemen come Sunday morning.

The waiter — possibly cook too judging from the stains on his apron — came out of the back, where Billy Ray thought the kitchen must be. He glanced at the preacher without welcome. "Yeah?" He was a smallish man of middle years, skinny except for a well-developed potbelly. He had a drooping mustache and a receding hairline.

41

"I'm Billy Ray Halstad, the new preacher." Billy Ray stood and extended his hand, smiling.

The waiter/cook blinked, hesitated for a moment and then shook Billy Ray's hand limply. "Yeah. How do." He did not introduce himself in return.

Billy Ray stood there awkwardly for a moment, then resumed his seat. "What, uh, do you have that would be cheap?"

"Meal's a quarter. San'wich, pie an' coffee would be fifteen cents. San'wich an' coffee ten cents." The prices were modest enough after what was charged in the mining camps. But then cash money would be dearer here with no high day wages bolstering the local economy. A mining man could expect to earn three dollars a day, but of course he needed that much to survive in towns where the cost of living was high. Billy Ray had no idea what a farmer or a cowhand could expect to earn.

"I'll have the sandwich and coffee please," Billy Ray said, mindful of the state of his purse at the moment.

"No pie?"

"No pie," he agreed.

The waiter/cook grunted and turned away without comment.

Billy Ray sighed. Strange place, this Purgatory City. It wasn't exactly the friendliest town he had ever come across.

But that was all right. He hoped. He waited patiently and in silence for his meal to be delivered, while at the other table the two old men continued to ignore him.

9

He lay tossing restlessly on the bare cot and mattress. He was a trifle cool, because he owned no blankets to bring with him and no one had thought to include those when the dugout was furnished, but apart from that he could not claim any discomfort.

The grass that had been stuffed into the mattress ticking was new. As yet there had been no weight placed on it to crush and pack the dried grass stems, and the mattress was plump and soft.

Really he had no room for complaint here. The rope-sprung cot was comfortable enough beneath him.

And he didn't even particularly mind being inside the dugout now. It was only partially underground and the rock facing on the walls let him convince himself that he was staying inside a low stone cabin rather than a hole in the ground.

So he hadn't that excuse either.

But here he lay, wide awake and miserable and unable to go to sleep after who knew how many hours of futile trying.

He had gone to bed early, tired from the stage journey, confused by his reception in Purgatory City and dispirited about being away from the mountains he had come to consider his home.

He hadn't even bothered to light a lamp, although the good people of his congregation had provided lamps and oil and matches, and the desk for him to work at if he wished.

That was the thing, really. Tonight he simply did not wish.

He'd thought to escape into sleep, and now he could not sleep either.

For a time he thought that might be because he had no pillow. He was accustomed to using a pillow. So he wadded his spare clothing inside his suit coat and used that as a pillow. It should suffice until he could find some scraps of cloth and make a proper pillow.

But that didn't do any good either.

Still he lay wide awake and tossing atop the soft mattress, the sort-of pillow tucked under his neck, with no sound or disturbance to bother him.

Still he couldn't sleep.

He *never* had trouble getting to sleep. Never. Until tonight.

Tonight the more he fretted about it the more awake he became. And the longer he lay awake in the intense darkness of the silent dugout the more tired and anxious for sleep he became.

He was exhausted. He *wanted* to sleep. He just couldn't.

Billy Ray laced his hands behind his neck and stared toward the dark, unseen roof overhead.

He knew what he ought to do, of course. Really he did.

If he couldn't sleep he should occupy himself constructively by spending this quiet, alone time in prayer.

But somehow he could not do that either.

It wasn't that he didn't try.

He lay alone in the darkness and mouthed the words that he knew he should say.

But that was all they were. Words. Without feeling. Without meaning.

Most of all they were words without that sense of *connection* that prayer was supposed to bring.

They were only words mumbled into the night. They went nowhere. They reached no ears but his own.

He could feel the emptiness of his words just as acutely as he could feel his own fatigue.

46

He knew that his words reached no higher than the roof of this dugout.

There was no sense of communion with God here. No feeling that his words — he couldn't even think of them as being prayer, not truly — were heard, much less heeded.

At this moment Billy Ray did not feel like a preacher who was capable of ministering to a flock. Even though that was why he had come here. Why he had agreed to take these folks' pay.

Right now he felt anything but like a preacher.

Right now he was only a man, alone in the night in a strange and unwelcoming place.

Right now not even the Lord was here to help him.

All the warm flood of salvation that he remembered so well . . . remembered but could not call back upon command . . . was simply . . . *gone.*

All the leaping joy, all the soaring of the spirit, all the happiness and love and warmth . . . they just weren't *there.*

And he missed them.

Dear God, how he missed them.

And he did not know how to call them back now that they had deserted him.

Billy Ray's belly was still full from the meal he had purchased.

But his soul was empty.

It was a hunger he did not know how to ease.

He lay there in the night, awake and hungering, for a very long time.

10

He had no idea what time they expected services to start on Sunday morning. No one bothered to tell him.

Billy Ray stayed up late Saturday night preparing a sermon on beginnings, drawing his text out of John and Second Thessalonians, but mostly out of the 111th Psalm where it said in the last verse that "The fear of the Lord is the beginning of wisdom . . ." and so on.

Billy Ray was kind of proud of being able to use Old Testament verses for his texts now. When he started out he mostly concentrated on the New Testament. And not even all of that, since his first Bible had a lot of pages missing from it. The past year or so he'd been spending more of his reading time on the early books and especially the Psalms, and he'd come to really like them.

His new Bible had a concordance in the back. He couldn't figure out now how he'd ever gotten along without one. Although he had.

Now it was easier. He wanted to say something about beginnings, so he looked up the word "beginning" in the concordance pages, and there the references were, listed right out for him from "In the beginning God created . . ." right at the very front and running on through to the last one listed, which was Revelation 1:8, the "Alpha and Omega" passage. Neat.

Billy Ray wrote his sermons out now, another thing he never used to do but had started once he figured he should be more professional about his preaching, now that he was being paid regular to head a real congregation.

He worked on his sermon until late Saturday and then was up by dawn. Not long after, he was sitting in the church, waiting for the folks to arrive.

Whenever they showed up he wanted to be ready for them.

The first wagons started rolling in by seven or seven-thirty, and the last of them by eight or thereabouts.

The only people he recognized, of course, were Ad and Norma Smits and Eli Pieck. Except for them it was all a blur of names and faces that would take some time to sort out into real people that he would know and remember.

Once they were all in place there seemed to be thirty-odd folks on hand for Billy Ray's first preaching in Purgatory City, the bunch of them divided along lines he couldn't quite follow yet into twelve families. Which explained the twelve dollar a month salary they'd promised. A dollar a family a month.

One thing he did notice right off from among all the new names and faces, and that was that there didn't seem to be a single marriageable and unattached female among them. Not a good-looking one nor even a plain girl beyond pigtail age. He couldn't help feeling a little disappointed by that discovery. The older farmers — which they all of them seemed to be here, no cowboys or ranchmen among them — ran strong to male children.

Since there wasn't any pulpit for him to get behind, Billy Ray sat up front on a stool he carried over from the dugout. He endured the greetings and the handshakes and the confusions of the many introductions, and smiled and smiled and smiled, and finally Brother Eli Pieck came up and let him know that everybody was on hand if he wanted to get started.

Brother Pieck resumed his seat on the crowded front-row bench, and the congregation quieted down. Billy Ray commenced to get dry in the throat and scared.

Right at that moment he didn't know what he was *doing* here.

He felt like a fraud. A complete dang fraud. And if he hadn't had a sermon already written down he wouldn't have had a thing to say to all these people.

"Howdy," he said in a voice that surprised him for being so loud and steady. "Thanks for bringing me here. And thank you too for all you did to set me up in the, uh, manse over there." He tried to smile and wasn't sure if he was bringing it off or not.

Lordy, but he did wish he had a pulpit up here to shelter behind.

He swallowed hard, remembering to keep his smile in place, and roared, "Are we all ready to praise the Lord today?" and everybody smiled back at him and a few folks shouted and a woman in the middle row on the right side, his right that is, waved her hands in the air, and it was all a little better after that.

But if it hadn't been for his written-down sermon he never would have been able to recall afterward just what it was he spoke on that first Sunday in his new church.

Assuming, that is, that he followed the written part — but he surely must have or he couldn't have gotten through the long morning.

11

Billy Ray felt wrung out. Sweaty and limp and exhausted, and the whole past morning was a blur. But it was over with now and everybody was filing out and shaking his hand and introducing themselves all over again, and this time a few of the names were starting to take hold.

The tall man with the sickly-looking wife was Andrews — Claude? or maybe it was that the wife was Claudia, he couldn't recall now — who had supplied the wagon the other day after Brother Pieck and the Smitses had had a breakdown.

And the gray-haired man with the surly, pouty-looking son was Harold Krohn. The boy was Jerry. Billy Ray remembered him because he spent most of his time during the service pestering a little girl on the bench in front of him. Jerry Krohn was a husky eighteen or so, and the little girl he'd been prodding in the back was ten or eleven. Billy Ray thought he remembered that her name was

Emmy. He couldn't recall who her folks were but he was sure of their faces now.

It was all most confusing.

"Fine sermon."

"Very nice."

"Thank you."

It all ran together in his mind, as the folks shook his hand and passed out toward the parked farm wagons scattered at their hitch weights on the bare, dusty ground in front of the church building. They'd all come in wagons. There wasn't a single one of them on a saddle horse that he could see, and no one lived close enough to have walked.

"Thank you, Reverend."

"Thank you, sister." His cheeks hurt from smiling so much this morning. And from not really meaning it very much of the time. "Pleasure to meet you, brother." "You take care, little lady." "See you next Sunday, son." "Pleasure to meet you, sister."

He smiled and shook hands and was conscious that his stomach was aching now from hunger. He'd been too nervous and in too much of a hurry to take time for breakfast earlier.

Brother Pieck and Brother Smits, he noticed, were holding back to be the last ones out, although Mrs. Smits had gone ahead to their wagon already.

They waited until everyone else was out of earshot before they came out.

Most of the wagons, Billy Ray noticed, turned toward the town when they left the church. Apparently the farmers used this weekly trip to town as their opportunity to do any shopping they needed done. There seemed to be no lunch grounds established, although it would have been a nice habit to adopt; perhaps somewhere down along the river where it would be cool and shady and pleasant for folks to get together and have box dinners, before they turned toward their homes and the labors of their work-week. It was something he would have to think about proposing in the future.

"Gentlemen," Billy Ray said when Brother Pieck and Brother Smits finally approached him.

"Fine sermon, Reverend," Brother Pieck said.

"Mild, though," Brother Smits said. "Psalms 111. Your own text, Reverend. 'He hath given meat unto them that fear him . . .' Verse Five, Reverend. And in Verse Ten, 'The fear of the Lord is the beginning of wisdom.' Not much fear in the way you put it this mornin', Reverend." Brother Smits used a thumbnail to pick something out of his front teeth and gave Billy Ray a baleful look. "The way is harsh, Reverend. We need remindin' of that. Harsh is the way o' the Lord. Harsh is the way o' man too. Man needs t' learn t' tremble before the Lord."

"Yes, well, thank you for reminding me of that, Brother Smits."

"My duty as your deacon, Reverend."

"Yes, well, thank you."

Smits shook Billy Ray's hand solemnly and marched off to join his wife.

"Are you settling in well, Reverend?" Pieck asked.

"Fine, thank you." The response was automatic and unthinking. As for the truthfulness of the statement, well, that remained to be seen.

Pieck hesitated for a moment, then smiled. "See you next Sunday, Reverend." He offered his hand and turned toward the last wagon on the grounds.

Billy Ray felt lonely after Brother Pieck drove away toward Purgatory City.

It was odd, but in all his life he could not recall ever having felt lonesome before. Not until he came here. Always before there had been others around whom he knew and who knew him. Family, friends, coworkers. Someone.

Now he felt very much alone.

With a sigh that had nothing to do with relief over the fact that his first sermon was successfully concluded, he turned and went back inside the rickety, sagging church building to collect his stool and carry it back to the dugout that was now his home.

12

After all the excitement of anticipation before the service, Sunday afternoon was a letdown.

Billy Ray was used to *doing* stuff. Getting out and talking to people, seeing to their needs, praying with them, listening to their problems and to their triumphs. Being *with* people.

Not now, by golly. These farmers came to church, listened quietly and then drove away.

Oh, they were pleasant enough. They were polite. They seemed like really nice folks.

But they weren't big on hanging around afterward to chat and mingle and socialize.

Billy Ray sure wished they were.

The church and the area around it seemed emptier now, somehow, than it had during the past couple days.

It occurred to him that nobody had wanted to invite him home for dinner. Nobody suggested he call on them. Hey, nobody even said where they lived in case he wanted to come see them. They all lived someplace else, and he didn't even know where.

Not that he would have had any way to *get* anyplace else if he ever *was* invited. Unless some of them lived within walking distance, that is. But still . . .

He sighed again and looked around the inside of the church building.

Shucks, there wasn't even a mess to clean up after the congregation left.

Except for the benches having been moved a few inches this way or that and needing to be straightened into line again, you couldn't hardly tell anyone had been there. A once-over with a broom, and the place would look like it hadn't been used in ages.

Even the children hadn't dropped any scribbles or hastily passed notes for him to pick up and chuckle over.

He looked overhead toward the clouds so clearly visible through the gaps in the roof, then out through the cracks in the walls. There really wasn't anything for him to do here. Heck, there weren't any hymnals to pick up and store away.

Music, he thought. He really missed having music. That was one of the things he'd intended to talk with the folks about after church — putting a choir together. But nobody had stayed around long enough for him to bring it up.

Next Sunday, he decided. He'd just talk about it during the service. Then they'd *have* to listen. He nodded firmly, that minor decision reached, and fetched his stool to take back to the dugout where it belonged.

The empty, silent dugout wasn't any more cheerily welcoming than the empty church building was, and for some reason he simply couldn't face the idea of spending Sunday afternoon alone inside the dark, cool little dwelling.

He couldn't afford to buy another meal out, of course. He only had a little cash left and no idea when he would be paid here. Probably not until he had been on the job a full month, he guessed. He certainly couldn't afford to squander what little he had on prepared foods.

But he supposed he could take a stroll into town. Get a drink of water free from the town well. See folks. Maybe find someone to talk to.

That would beat sitting around feeling homesick and lonesome.

He left his Bible on the little work desk, put his cap back on and wandered slowly in the direction of Purgatory City.

61

13

Now that was a strange thing, Billy Ray reflected, as he entered the business section of the town.

All the stores were open and doing some business, but about the only folks he saw doing any of that business were the people of his own congregation. Not all of them had come into town after services, but most of them had, it looked like.

Just about all the faces he saw on the street today he recognized. And most of them seemed to be the children who just a little while ago had been inside his church. Their parents likely were indoors doing whatever buying was needed for the week to come.

Yesterday, he recalled, there had been quite a bit of traffic into and out of Purgatory City. Saturday shoppers, a few of them driving light wagons but most of them mounted horseback. And most of them dressed in the boots and spurs and big hats that said they were cowboys — No, he corrected himself, not cowboys but cowhands. He'd been told by some fellas in Blue Gorge who should know such things that cowhands didn't like to be called cow*boys*, for some reason or other. Not that Billy Ray cared one way or another, but it was the sort of thing he'd told himself to make note of once he learned he would be moving down here onto the plains.

Anyway, yesterday the town had been full up and roaring with cowhands and cattlemen. He'd been able to hear the sounds of their revelry late into the night, while he was up working on the morning's sermon.

Today, he saw, there wasn't hardly a cowboy — cowhand, darn it — in sight. What of them were left in town were probably in a long, low-roofed log building at the far end of town. That place, set kind of off to itself a little piece, had a bunch of bored, tail-twitching saddle horses tied to a rail in front.

Billy Ray could pretty much guess what kind of place that one was, of course. He'd been a bit of a hell-raiser himself up until he went and got saved, and he remembered how it'd been. Payday Saturday night was for the purpose of getting drunk and getting rid of your pay in that and certain other

63

ways, at least as far as he'd known at the time. Apparently cowhands weren't a whole lot different from miners when it came to Saturday nights.

But now in the broad daylight of Sunday afternoon there wasn't any movement on the street except for the farmers from Billy Ray's congregation. The cowhands, what ones of them were still in town, were staying to themselves in Purgatory City's one and only slop joint.

It reminded him, now that he thought on it, how the quality folks in Blue Gorge would kind of disappear when the working stiffs drew their pay and took over the town for the evening and next day.

Yet this seemed a bit backside-to, because it was the cowhands who were the rowdy, loose-money crowd of single fellas, and the farmers that were the settled family men. Yet it was the farmers who mostly had the town to themselves on Sunday afternoon, while the cowhands just held sway on Saturday night.

Sure was different down here, Billy Ray concluded.

He went over to the town well and got his drink of cool, refreshing water that didn't cost him anything, and then ambled down to Mr. Ayres's mercantile simply because it

64

was the only place in town that he knew. There were other businesses open this afternoon, but he was at least a little bit familiar with Mr. Ayres's place. And on his way over he'd decided that he really needed some crackers and hard cheese to add to his larder. Both of those were cheap and went a long way toward filling a man.

There was a wagon tied outside the mercantile. Billy Ray didn't recognize the wagon, but the little girl sitting in it was Emmy Something-or-other, who had been the object of Jerry Krohn's pestering earlier.

"Hello, Emmy."

"H'lo, Reverend."

"Let me see now, your last name is . . . ?"

"Elwick, Reverend." She looked like she didn't know whether to turn shy or be pleased by the attention.

"Oh, yes. And your daddy is . . . ?"

"Will, Reverend. Short for William. And my mama's name is Ethel."

"Thank you." He winked at her, and she giggled. She and the new preacher shared a kind of secret. And she had been able to help him out with something.

"Could I ask you something, Reverend?"

"Sure, Emmy. You can ask me anything you like."

"But you wouldn't . . . I mean . . . ?"

"I won't tell anybody if you don't want me to."

"Promise?"

He nodded solemnly.

"Okay." She paused for a moment and took a deep breath, then opened her mouth to speak.

She clamped it tight shut again, and her eyes shifted past Billy Ray's shoulder. He turned and saw her parents Will and Ethel coming out of the store. Will had his arms full of sacks, and Ethel was struggling with the weight of a bag of some loose, bulky stuff that was probably flour or cornmeal.

Billy Ray hurried onto the board sidewalk to take the bag from her and carry it to the back of the wagon.

He looked at Emmy, but the little girl gave him an abrupt, barely perceptible shake of her head.

Whatever it was she wanted to discuss, she didn't want to talk about it with her parents listening in. Billy Ray nodded again to show her he understood, and silently mouthed, "Later." Emmy seemed relieved.

Will Elwick greeted Billy Ray but did not seem inclined to stop and visit. "Next week, Reverend." He went around to the side of the driving box and climbed onto the wagon without helping his wife onto her side of the seat. Ethel was left to collect the hitch weight from the draft horse's bit and put it onto the floorboards. Billy Ray helped her onto the seat, and Will shook out the driving lines.

"Good-bye, folks."

" 'Bye, Reverend," Ethel said.

Will put the horse into motion, and Emmy, behind her parents' backs, gave Billy Ray a small shrug and a smile. She waved to him as the rig pulled off down the street toward the east.

The call to this church, Billy Ray decided, wasn't at all what he had expected when he agreed to come here.

He watched the Elwick wagon out of sight, then turned to go inside Walker Ayres's store and buy his cheese and crackers.

14

As before, Walker Ayres was efficient but unsmiling. The merchant gave the impression of a man who would take Billy Ray's money but did not particularly care if he had the preacher's trade or not. Even though he knew perfectly good and well who and what Billy Ray was, there was no greeting, no outward sign of recognition. For all the warmth Ayres displayed, this might have been a big city store where strangers were common and disinterest the norm.

Ayres, Billy Ray noted, had shaved since the last time Billy Ray was in the store, but he hadn't done it this morning.

There was a faint, gray mat of fur on the merchant's jowls again. Apparently Ayres shaved for Saturdays but not for Sundays.

"It's a pleasure to see you looking so well on a fine Sabbath afternoon, Mr. Ayres," Billy Ray said cheerfully. He smiled but this time did not push it so far as to extend a hand to the storekeeper. No point in putting either of them through that awkwardness again.

Ayres grunted and shifted his eyes elsewhere.

"I need some groceries, Mr. Ayres." The storekeeper nodded, examining his fingernails. "Ten cents worth of cheese, I think. And, oh, two cents of those hard crackers?"

Ayres cleared his throat, looked like he wanted to spit but didn't. He left his stool and went behind a tall, glass-front display case to fetch out a wheel of yellow cheese and a knife.

Billy Ray stood idly examining a jar of hard candies on top of the display case. The red and blue and green and yellow confections were like bright, sweet gems inside the glass. Billy Ray thought that perhaps, after he was paid and could afford a bit extra, perhaps he could start a Sunday School class for the children and reward progress with a treat. Perhaps he could . . .

There was a commotion in the street outside. A stamping of hooves and a loud whinny, followed by a loud, sharp curse that pierced the quiet of the afternoon. Ayres looked up from the cheese wheel for a moment, then quickly down again.

Billy Ray glanced first at Ayres, then turned and went to the doorway.

Whoever had started cussing was still doing it. The male voice was harsh and nasty and cutting.

In the street just outside Ayres's store, Billy Ray could see a farm wagon and beside it a horse and rider. He recognized the couple in the wagon. They were the youngest members of his congregation, a man and wife whose names he did not recall yet, and with them a wide-eyed, frightened child of two or three.

The horseman who continued to loudly upbraid them with a monotonously repeated string of curses was a young man no older and no larger than the pasty-faced farmer on the wagon seat. But the cowboy seemed much the larger, perhaps because of the blued-steel revolver that rode in a holster snug and high against his hip.

The cowboy was actually carrying a gun. Billy Ray could hardly believe that. Despite all the wild and lurid tales in the magazines and dime novels of the day, in all his years in mountain mining communities Billy Ray doubted he had ever seen anyone except a peace officer who wore a revolver on his hip. He'd known a few men who owned rifles and hunted with them. And one of the boys who used to work at the Chagra No. 1 Mine had a fist-sized, nickel-plated pistol that he

70

used to carry in his pocket on Saturday nights. But Billy Ray had quite honestly never seen a revolver worn openly like this before. Seeing this cowboy wearing one now was like seeing some fiction off of a magazine illustration spring to life.

The young farmer on the wagon seat was trying to stammer an apology or something. The furious cowboy couldn't hear any of that for his own loudly profane blustering.

Billy Ray couldn't help but notice that the farmer's young wife was blushing furiously, trying to cover the child's ears and to ignore the ugly, shouted words.

The child was crying by now, probably upset more by its mother's reaction than by the language the cowboy was using.

The whole thing seemed quite a mess.

Billy Ray sauntered smiling into the middle of it.

"Brother. Sister." He touched the brim of his cap toward the young wife and reached out to chuck the little one under the chin. He looked up at the cowboy, looming eight feet tall above him on the back of an exceptionally handsome bay horse. "Hello." Still smiling, he reached up to extend his hand. "I'm Billy Ray Halstad. And who might you be?"

The cowboy stopped his flow of invective

and blinked. He automatically responded to the offered handshake with a gesture of his own hand, then thought better of it and snatched his gloved hand back. He seemed confused now.

Billy Ray kept smiling up at him. "And your name is . . . ?"

The cowboy looked unhappily back and forth between Billy Ray and the farmer.

"His name is Trumaine," the farmer said. "Derek Trumaine." The tone of his voice made it an accusation rather than an introduction. And it was definitely the wrong thing for him to have said, or at least the worst possible timing.

Derek Trumaine's face darkened with a rush of renewed anger, and he shifted his attention from Billy Ray to the young man on the wagon. "You son of a bitch!"

The farmer's wife covered the child's ears again and dragged the now crying youngster onto her lap.

"You tried to kill my horse, damn you."

"You tried to . . ."

"Both of you calm down," Billy Ray snapped.

Both men stopped their shouting and looked at him.

"Now dang it anyway," Billy Ray said. "I don't know what happened here, but . . . no, just shut up a minute, the both of you . . . as I was saying, dang it, I don't know what's happened here, but I'm willing to bet neither one of you does either, and . . ."

"This idiot son of a bitch of a clodhopper pulled his rig right out in front of me, an' . . ."

"This fool was racing out of control down the street, and . . ."

"Both of you hush up," Billy Ray said calmly. "It's perfectly obvious that what you had here was a near accident and that nobody did anything with deliberate intent. Nobody was hurt, so what's the big fuss about?"

"This son of a bitch . . ."

"This fool . . ."

Billy Ray chuckled and gave the wife a grin and a wink. She gave him a weak, tentative smile in return. "Get fussed up kinda easy, don't they?"

The farmer grunted and glared out across the broad back of his draft horse. The cowboy turned his head away and spat.

Billy Ray couldn't help but wonder if maybe there was something else between these two very different men. The wife, perhaps? She was certainly pretty enough. And looked like she must have been even prettier before motherhood and the hardships of farm life took the color from her cheeks. Both men were of about the same age. It wasn't impossible that both of them might have been courting her once. There could have been an old animosity remaining from that.

He was just guessing, of course, but both men reacted once he brought the woman back to their attention.

He tipped his cap to the lady again, "Ma'am."

"Reverend." She nodded. At this point she looked just the tiniest bit pleased by the whole thing, Billy Ray thought. Just a touch proud. As if flattered that the two still cared to fuss over her? "We'd best drive on, Sammy."

Sammy. Billy Ray remembered now. Sam and Charity Martin. He thought they were related somehow to the Smits family, though he wasn't sure what the connection was. At least they'd been sitting together during services in a manner that said they were family.

"Son of a bitch," Trumaine mumbled, though Billy Ray couldn't decide if the epithet was directed toward Sam Martin in particular or was a complaint uttered in general.

Martin glanced briefly and none too kindly toward Trumaine, and put his rig into motion. He didn't look at Billy Ray again, but Charity Martin did. She gave him a look that combined gratitude with pleasure, and sat on the wagon seat with her chin held high and her child clutched to her, while Sam drove off toward the east.

Trumaine grunted something that Billy Ray couldn't hear and turned his bay in the opposite direction, out toward the end of town where the slop joint was. He didn't look at Billy Ray either.

"Nice to've met you," Billy Ray said to the horseman's back, but Trumaine ignored him.

Billy Ray grinned and walked back inside Walker Ayres's store. The merchant was seated on his stool behind the counter, but there was something in his posture that suggested he'd just barely gotten back to the seat. And Billy Ray noted that the cheese and a generous heap of hard crackers hadn't yet been wrapped. They were tumbled loose on a sheet of paper on the counter.

"Twelve cents," Ayres said as he folded the paper and tied it into a bundle for easy carrying.

Billy Ray paid and picked up his package. "And I thank you very much, Mr. Ayres."

Ayres turned away without answering, and fumbled with something on a shelf so his back was to Billy Ray.

15

Billy Ray was whistling. His shoulder muscles felt like there were waves of wild fire shooting through them, and his hands hurt and he was sticky with sweat and runny mud, but really he felt pretty good. He'd almost forgotten the way hard, physical labor felt. It wasn't, by golly, bad.

His intention first thing Monday morning had been to build an earth sump near the church so he could carry water from the river, mix it with dirt there on the spot and then use that to caulk the wide gaps between the warped logs of the church walls.

That notion hadn't turned out so well. It seemed the earth where the church was built was hard, rock-filled clay that was impossible to dig with the broken coal scoop Billy Ray retrieved from the trash dump, so he had to shift his operation down beside the riverbank to where the dirt was dark and loamy and much, much easier to dig.

He built his dirt-walled sump there and

transferred water into it to make mud. Now he was using a piece of splintered shingle to chop leaves and bits of grass into the mud, the idea being that the loose woodlot litter would act as a binder when the mud dried. He'd gotten his recipe for the mixture out of Exodus, the part where the king of Egypt was trying to mess up Moses by making it impossible for the people to make the bricks right, saying they couldn't have any straw to use in them.

Once he got the mortar made he'd have to lug it over to the church and put it on quick before it dried.

It was heavy work but nothing that a man with time on his hands couldn't accomplish.

And it sure would make a difference in the comfort inside the church, particularly come winter when the cold air would whip through those cracks if something wasn't done about it now.

Yesterday afternoon he'd given the church building a good looking-over. The corners seemed sturdy enough, he discovered, and the old logs were dried and warped but not in as much danger of falling down as they looked.

What he figured to do was to tackle this first and chink up the walls.

After that he could decide what to do with

the roof. That was really the weakest and poorest part of the structure. But he could worry about it when the walls were done.

He sighed, thinking about the dang roof. The truth of the matter was that Billy Ray was scared to death of heights. The thought of having to climb onto that shaky, rickety, no-account roof was already worrying him.

This here was the *easy* part. The part that could be done while he was standing on the ground.

He flexed his shoulders to try and ease them a little, then bent back over his over-grown mud pie, tossed another handful of leaves on top of the mess and began whacking and pounding at it with the edge of the shingle.

Billy Ray hoped the Lord knew what He was doing when it came to making mortar, because His servant dang sure didn't.

"Ooo-whee." It felt so good to be able to quit that it almost made the pain worth-while.

His shoulders and arms were raw pain, and his hands had blistered, and the blisters had broken so many times already that the insides of them looked like beefsteak.

But he had two thirds of the north wall freshly caulked, all the gaps and chinks filled with fresh mortar that was drying nice.

Another week or so and there wouldn't be the least bit of wind could get through.

"Shee-oot, yes," he said to the birds that were flitting through the cottonwood branches over his head.

It was coming evening, the air already cool, a slight breeze rising now that he no longer needed it.

There were all manner of little-bitty birds flocking in to the trees along the river, ready to roost for the night. Billy Ray didn't know one bird from another, but he kind of liked seeing them here. There weren't very many birds up in the high country that he was used to, and this bunch of them down on the plains were something of a treat.

There was a line of clouds off to the west, off toward the distant, hidden mountains, and the setting sun that was long since out of sight itself had the undersides of them lit up in reds and golds and yellows.

This country was kind of pretty in its own way, even if it wasn't anything like so spectacular as the big peaks.

One thing that *wasn't* so pretty right now was Billy Ray Halstad. He wrinkled his nose and made a face. He was a sweaty, muddy mess, and he could smell himself. He'd been around hard-worked mules that smelled better than he did right now. He sniffed again, confirming it, and realized he'd better wash off some before he went back to the dugout for supper and a rest.

Good thing the river was handy. Of course he might cause a problem for anybody wanting to use the water downstream, but he figured he'd just have to chance that. He kicked his shoes off, thought about removing his socks and trousers and decided he'd probably better wash them too if he was going to be in the water anyhow.

Why not?

He picked his way carefully down the bank toward the water, the soles of his feet tender and ouchy on the rocks and twigs on the ground.

He was knee-deep in the cold water when he heard a thrashing of branches from something large and heavy moving through the brush only a few yards away.

Bear, was his first, chilling thought.

There were plenty of bears in the mountains, and practically everybody Billy Ray knew was scared of them.

He froze in place.

He heard a loud, moist "whuff" of deep, fluttering breath, and some more thrashing in the brush.

It was a bear sure enough.

nce that if you
ee you, but
tried to

ou were
l and lay
could make
ed real still

hrill laugh, and
scared fish-belly
et red.

the sound
air, and
eps down
r.

glossy
d com-
fort it
reins,
e wa-

her
nd
hat
a

16

"You . . . startled me."

"So I noticed." She laughed,
bright and clear on the evening
bumped her horse the final few st
the bank so it could reach the wate

The animal was a small-boned
coated, pale red creature that seeme
pletely unperturbed by the discom
had just caused. The girl loosened her
and the horse dropped its muzzle to th
ter's surface to drink.

Obviously that was what had brough
here. And just as obviously it was the so
of the horse moving through the brush t
Billy Ray had mistaken for the noises o
bear approaching behind him.

The knowledge only helped make hir
feel all the more foolish. He must have
jumped two feet when he was trying so hard
to be still.

"Sorry," she said. "I didn't mean to sneak
up on you. But there's never anyone around

here. Hardly ever, anyway."

"No, it's . . . my fault. I'm sure." He didn't quite see how that was supposed to be so. But it seemed the right thing to say.

The girl laughed again and reached down to stroke the horse's neck.

The red horse was an uncommonly pretty thing.

But then so was its rider.

The girl was so very pretty that Billy Ray found himself tongue-tied.

For some reason this made all the more acute his embarrassment at having her find him here all filthy dirty and sweaty, and with his shirt and shoes off.

The girl and the horse were only a few yards away. Billy Ray hoped the failing light would keep her from getting a good look at him. Although it didn't, in fact, keep him from getting a perfectly good look at her.

She was . . . lovely. Really. A little bit of a thing with long hair that she was wearing loose, probably to accommodate the wide-brimmed, flat-crowned hat that was perched jauntily on her head and kept in place by a ribbon. Billy Ray hadn't seen a girl wear her hair loose in . . . well, it had been a very long time ago when he'd last seen such. And under circumstances that no preacher would allow himself to be in.

83

This girl was small and perky, with a heart-shaped face and huge eyes and a rounded little point of chin and . . . never mind the rest. Billy Ray tried not to pay attention to how close-cut her shirtwaist was.

She had a loose, casual riding seat that made her look like she had been born in a saddle. The saddle, he noted, was as unusual as her hairstyle. It was a stock seat built small to accommodate her size, but otherwise very much like an ordinary cowhand's saddle. And she rode it astride, her dark brown skirt cut very full and somehow divided in the middle so she could sit on the horse like a man would.

Billy Ray was sure he'd never before seen a woman ride any way but sidesaddle, and that not very often.

She wore high-topped boots that effectively kept her from showing anything she shouldn't. But he couldn't help noticing that the boots were awfully small at the ankle and calf, which meant that what was inside them was trim and shapely too.

He swallowed, his throat dry, and waded back to the bank to retrieve his shirt. He pulled it on quickly.

"I've disrupted your bath. I really am sorry."

"No, it's . . . uh . . . all right."

"Forgive me?" She smiled, probably already guessing that he would forgive her quite nearly anything without her even having to ask. She was that kind of girl. He didn't see how it would be possible for anyone to be angry with her even if she did something to deserve anger. And she certainly hadn't done anything like that here. All she wanted was to give the horse a drink.

He nodded.

"I don't know you, so you must be the new preacher," she suggested.

It occurred to him, very much too late, that it was his obligation to introduce himself and not the other way around.

"Oh, uh, yes, miss." He put a hand up, intending to remove his cap, then remembered that he wasn't wearing one. The cap was dangling from a tree limb near his mud sump. "I'm Billy Ray Halstad."

"Pleasure to meet you, Reverend." The horse was done getting its drink. She retrieved the reins and pulled it around to the bank so it was still standing in the water at the river's edge, but was again quite close.

"Just Billy Ray," he said quickly.

She smiled. "I'm Denise Trumaine, Just Billy Ray." She leaned down and offered her hand. He barely touched her fingertips, and at that was conscious of how dirty he was after working with the mortar all day.

"My pleasure, Miss . . . oh. Of course. It would be Missus, wouldn't it. I mean, I met a young gentleman yesterday. Derek Trumaine? He must be your husband."

Denise made a sour face and then laughed. "Derek? Pity the poor girl he finally decides on. He's my brother. And it is *Miss* Trumaine, sir. The old maid of Purgatory City."

"I can't believe that." She looked to be no more than twenty at the outside.

"Gallant of you to say so, I'm sure, Just Billy Ray, but the fact remains . . ." She gave him a long, sad face, then laughed again. "No matter. Someday I'll find someone rich enough for Daddy to approve of." She giggled. "Of course that wonderful someone will no doubt be old and fat and reek of cigar smoke. But he'll have Daddy's approval. That will be the important thing."

Billy Ray couldn't decide if Miss Trumaine was playing or if she was being halfway serious with him. He concluded it would probably be best if he didn't try to figure that one out for the time being.

"Whoever the lucky fellow is," he said, "I'm sure it will be the person God has in mind just for you."

Her bright, gay expression changed and

just for a moment she gave him a close, searching, quite serious look. The seriousness lasted only for a moment, however. Almost too brief for him to be sure he'd seen it. Then she was smiling again, her voice light and insubstantial. "A promise from the pulpit, Just Billy Ray?"

"No," he told her. "The only real promise you can get from a pulpit is for salvation. The rest you kind of have to help out with."

Again, but only for an instant, he could see seriousness in her eyes.

"Pooh," she said gaily. "And there I was getting my hopes up. Oh, well. Silly me." She giggled and patted the horse's neck. "I suppose I shall have to go back to my fears of a fat knight with tarnished armor, shan't I?"

"Do you always do this?"

"Do what?"

"Hide behind a simper and a giggle?"

That was an *awful* thing for him to have said. He'd no sooner said it than he wished he had bitten his tongue instead.

Instead of being angry with him, though, Denise looked startled. She drew back so sharply in her seat that the horse felt the motion and backed away, its hocks swirling through the slow-moving water.

"I'm sorry," he said quickly but too late.

"I have to go now," Denise said. "I'm sorry I disrupted your bath, preacher."

Before he had a chance to properly apologize, she reined the horse away from him. It lurched out of the water to the solid footing on the bank, and the girl spurred it through the brush to open ground beneath the cottonwoods. It broke into a swift lope and disappeared from sight in the shadows that now lined the river.

"Damn," Billy Ray breathed. The word came out so suddenly that he didn't have time to stop it, and he felt so annoyed at the moment that he didn't even apologize for using it.

He took his shirt off and again waded out into the water, this time not caring that the water was cold and uncomfortable.

What an unusual girl, he was thinking. And so extraordinarily pretty.

It was probably a very good thing that the river water *was* so cold.

17

Sore muscles and physical exhaustion do *not* help a fellow get to sleep, no matter that you'd think they would. Billy Ray lay awake a long time that night.

But he had to admit that he wasn't thinking about all the work that needed doing on the church building. Nor even about all the work that needed doing *with* the church. With, that is, the congregation.

What he kept thinking about was Denise Trumaine and how pretty she was and, perhaps even more than that, how deep-down serious she was underneath the laughing front she put on.

Oh, she did seem lighthearted and happy enough, really. But there was a lot more to her than that. Billy Ray could sense it as much as he'd been able to see it in those few brief glimpses she'd shown him.

There was something about her.

And . . . dang it . . . he was preaching for a living. But that didn't mean he wasn't a man too. And he just couldn't help but respond to a girl as pretty as Denise like any other man would have to.

He sighed. Folks kind of got the idea that preachers weren't entirely human. That they were or they should be — or, the way some insisted on seeing it, that they themselves *thought* they were — something better than the ordinary guy.

Well, dang it, Billy Ray *was* an ordinary guy. The only thing different between him and the next guy was that Billy Ray'd been saved and maybe that next fellow hadn't been. But that right there was the only dang difference.

He sighed again into the lonely emptiness of the dark dugout.

The truth of it, really, was that maybe he was *too* ordinary.

Maybe those folks who set preachers apart from the common herd of humanity had something right after all.

Maybe preachers *should* be better than everybody else.

And if that was so, well maybe, just maybe, Billy Ray Halstad had gotten into the wrong line of work here.

Maybe he really shouldn't make himself out to be a preacher man. And then lie here in a narrow bunk and think late into the night about a pretty girl he'd just barely met.

Billy Ray wished he had someone he could talk to about these things. Preferably a preacher. A really sharp and knowledgeable preacher. That was probably what he really needed. But in the whole of Purgatory City and the countryside around it there wasn't a soul he knew well enough to go and talk to about things like this.

Heck, he was the guy *they* were supposed to come to and ask about *their* concerns.

And plain old Billy Ray — Just Billy Ray, she'd called him — he didn't know enough to answer his *own* dang questions, much less anybody else's.

He worried about that for a long, late time that night, and when it came light outside, and with it time to get up and working again, he had no more answers than he'd had to begin with, and was still weary and worn-out now in the bargain.

18

Billy Ray quit early the next afternoon. There was still a good hour or more of daylight left he could have worked in, but the truth was that he was about at the end of his rope for the day because of not sleeping worth a darn the night before.

He was still sore all over. That wouldn't ease up until he'd been laboring long enough to build some stamina into muscles that hadn't really been used hard for some time.

More than that, though, his head was pounding like some fool was using his temples as anvils, breaking ore samples on them.

His eyes felt gritty and his throat raw, and his hands burned like fire from all the broken blisters that were seeping and oozing on his palms.

He'd gotten quite a bit done though, by golly. More, in fact, than yesterday. Mostly that was because today he'd had his tools all figured out and the mud sump in place ready to go straight to work in, and because today he knew more about how to go about the chore he'd set for himself. Yesterday there had been a lot of figuring out to be done before he could accomplish much. Today he'd been able to jump to it and just work, without having to think about what to do before he could get to the doing of it.

By the time he knocked off for the day — no welcome end-of-shift whistle to tell him when, and no hot meal waiting for him in the boarding hall after the whistle blew — the whole north wall was finished, and he had about a third of the west wall done. Nearly belt-high on the west wall.

The church was starting to look pretty nice, with the fresh chinking between the logs to make the building look like it was really being used for something, instead of just standing there like an empty old eyesore.

By the time he got it all finished with a solid roof overhead, why, anybody driving by would be able to see that there was a real church in town. The way it was to begin with, it just looked abandoned.

He didn't want the congregation to see it that way anymore than he wanted passersby to get the wrong idea.

He used up the last of his third mix of mud-and-trash mortar, and called it quits for the day.

Going into the river to get a bath, he couldn't help but be the least bit hopeful that today again he'd be startled by bear noises behind him and turn and see Denise and that little red horse. But of course there wasn't any such luck. Not that he'd actually *expected* it. But . . .

He fussed at himself for being silly, washed away the mud and the sweat of the day's work and walked back out onto the riverbank to dry.

He didn't have much in the way of extra clothing to be changing in and out of, so he just let his clothes dry on him while the rest of him dried with them. Fortunately the plains air was dry itself and quickly took all the moisture it could reach. It was really a wonder the rivers themselves didn't dry up here. But then come to think of it he'd heard that the creeks and the smaller rivers sometimes did. That was something he could believe now, where before he would have thought it just a tall tale somebody was wanting to feed him.

He stacked his makeshift tools ready for tomorrow's work and started off toward the dugout.

The dang dugout, though, held no attraction for him.

There wasn't anything there to draw him except the prospect of a lonesome supper, and the hard work of mixing and carrying and applying mortar had pretty much taken his appetite away.

Practically in the middle of a stride he changed direction, angling away from the church and the dugout toward town. It was still early enough that some of the stores should be open.

It wasn't that he wanted to buy anything. Heck, he couldn't afford to be buying stuff all the time. It was just that he wanted to *talk* to somebody. It didn't hardly matter who he talked to or what about. Just . . . somebody. About anything.

Purgatory City on a Tuesday evening wasn't exactly a wide-open, booming operation.

There was one light buggy parked on the street in front of a shop that had a barber's striped pole out front, and there were a couple saddle horses tied here and there. Most of them were congregated near the café where he'd eaten that one time. Some of the businesses had already closed up for the day.

Billy Ray couldn't help thinking about the

folks who were able to finish their day's work and go home to a warm kitchen full of the good smells of supper, and family waiting for the man of the house to wash up and call them all together.

That wasn't the sort of thing he'd ever particularly thought about before, and certainly never with any sense of longing to have it for himself.

Now for some reason that idea seemed almighty attractive. Extra nice, somehow.

Billy Ray'd been out on his own, making his own way, usually surrounded by a bunch of other single fellas, in one mining camp or another . . . gosh, he could hardly remember when it'd been any different than that. It had been that long ago.

He could still remember it, though. Mostly what came to mind in his recollections was the smell of a warm, slightly smoky kitchen, with a soup pot bubbling on the stove and maybe the yeasty scent of something baking.

Now that he thought about it, he could remember the way bacon popped and smelled when it was frying, and bread hot out of the oven so that it steamed just a little when you broke it open, and the way fresh churned butter melted into a golden puddle when you slathered it thick on the hot, soft bread.

Funny how boarding house food or the stuff a bachelor threw together for himself never had that same kind of appeal.

Billy Ray realized what he was doing. He couldn't help but laugh at himself for it.

He was being dumb, was what he was doing here. Imagining things and getting all nostalgic and thinking fool thoughts that he had no right to.

Of course there were folks packing it in after a day's work and going home to supper. That's what family men did. And there wasn't anything about it that was more right or more wrong than what he was doing.

Everybody did what it was given them to do, and that was the long and the short of it.

And it just so happened that it wasn't given to Billy Ray Halstad to do like those other fellows here in town.

All he could properly expect was to do his level best with what *was* given him to do. And not fret himself with anything else.

He whistled his way down the street, randomly picking the tune of "Just As I Am," and since he really didn't know any other place or person he turned in at Mr. Ayres's mercantile, just to browse and maybe chat a bit if the merchant was willing.

19

He couldn't afford to buy anything, but that didn't prevent him from looking and thinking. His clothes weren't going to last too awfully long, what with working in mud and whatnot, so he examined the few things Mr. Ayres offered in that line, anticipating the time when he would be paid and perhaps be able to afford a new pair of trousers.

For some reason there were shelves of men's clothes on two opposite sides of the small store; sturdy Levi's, corduroy trousers and two pairs of flannel trousers on one shelf, and a selection of bib overalls completely on the other side of the place.

Billy Ray looked at the corduroys, thinking they should be good enough for everyday wear and should last well. He didn't price them, though. There was no point in that yet. In a month or thereabouts he could ask the price and hopefully buy a pair.

"Pickle?"

"Pardon me?"

"I asked do you want a pickle," Walker Ayres said. He managed to make his voice sound as sour as his product, like he was reluctant to put the words out onto the air, but his expression wasn't unkind.

"Oh, uh, thanks, but I can't really afford to buy anything."

Ayres scowled. "Didn't ask do you want t' buy one. Offered one. There's a difference." He cleared his throat noisily. "Fresh barrel. Got too many o' the damn things."

"Well . . . thank you." Billy Ray smiled at the storekeeper, who promptly looked away, like he was embarrassed or perhaps ashamed.

The pickles were huge, plump, green and yellow things floating in a brine that had an odor powerful enough to pucker you up five feet before you ever got to the barrel.

"Thanks," Billy Ray repeated. He politely selected one of the smaller pickles and bit into it. It was crisp enough to pop and crunch under his teeth and was tartly delicious. He grinned. "This is great."

Ayres frowned and examined the far wall of his store.

"Would you mind telling me something?"

Ayres grunted but didn't exactly answer.

"Have I done something to, um, offend people here?"

This time Ayres looked at him, but the man still didn't say anything. He looked at Billy Ray closely for a moment and then again looked away.

Billy Ray took another bite of pickle.

He wandered past the shelves of clothing to a rack of smaller shelving, where there were odds and ends of small products. He would be needing another cake of shaving soap soon. Hopefully the one he'd brought with him would last until he got paid. If it came to that he supposed he could shave with just hot water for a spell, if he had to.

Or grow a beard. He wondered if he might look more dignified with a beard. He'd never grown one before, not really, although when he'd first gone to the mining country he tried once. It had itched something awful and had grown in with a patch here and a tuft there, but not enough to really look much like a proper beard. Of course he'd been awfully young at the time. He just might want to think about trying it again here.

He fingered his chin, wondering if he just should go ahead and give it a try. If nothing else it would eliminate the nuisance of heating water to shave with every morning. Save on wood and water and trouble alike.

Yeah, it just might be worth trying once.

Have to start it on a Monday, though, so he wouldn't look any more scruffy than necessary the following Sunday morning.

Yeah, he just might try that.

He popped the last bite of pickle into his mouth, enjoying the crunch and the flavor both.

Mr. Ayres had turned so that his back was to Billy Ray. He was bent over on his stool, paring his fingernails with a penknife.

Now that was a man who was hard to figure out, Billy Ray reflected.

He thought about making another stab at conversation but was interrupted by the sound of a saddle horse stopping on the street outside. The animal came in at a hard run, slid to a stop just outside Ayres's store and snorted loudly. A moment later there was the sound of boot heels striking the board sidewalk, and Derek Trumaine sauntered in.

The cowboy — cow*hand*, Billy Ray corrected himself — seemed in no great hurry, despite the speed of his arrival.

Ayres turned and smiled. "H'lo, Derek."

"Evening, Mr. Ayres."

"Something I can do for you, Derek?"

"That shackle Papa was asking you about the other day?"

Ayres nodded. "I remember."

"Well, he said to tell you the weld didn't hold. He'd like you please to order him a new one."

"I'll have it out the first mail that goes, Derek. Tell him, though, that it'll be two weeks 'fore it gets here."

"Yes, sir, he knows that. Bubba is trying another weld to hold us the meanwhile, but Papa says we'd best count on a new one anyway."

"I'll have it for him quick as I can."

"Thank you, sir."

Billy Ray had been staring at Derek, not even thinking about being impolite. He was trying to decide if he could see a family resemblance between Derek and Denise, and couldn't, really, unless he wanted to fabricate one. Derek was much fairer haired but with weather-darkened skin. Both, though, were young and nice-looking. Maybe a little around the eyes and nose?

Derek glanced toward him and caught him looking. The young man's demeanor changed instantly. He had come into the store bright and cheerful. Now he looked like he'd just smelled something that had rotted. "What the hell are you starin' at?" he challenged.

Billy Ray smiled inoffensively. "Sorry."

Derek puffed up and looked ready to spit.

He balled his hands into fists and took two short, stiff-legged steps closer.

"I'd beat the crap outa you, mister, except it wouldn't be a contest."

Billy Ray smiled at Derek again.

That probably was the wrong thing to do, but he couldn't help it. He was thinking how absurd that statement was.

Derek only said it because Billy Ray was a preacher and could be expected to turn the other cheek. Heck, preachers were supposed to be meek and weak and not know how to mix it up.

Shee-oot, Billy Ray hadn't always been a preacher.

And if cowboys thought they knew something about scrapping, well, maybe they should spend a little time in a mining camp boarding house. Or better yet wander into a boom camp some payday Saturday night. Just see who it was left standing when the sawdust settled back onto the floor.

Billy Ray wasn't all that big, particularly. But he'd always considered himself big enough, by golly. And there hadn't been very dang-many times when he wasn't the fella still on his feet after a fracas.

Still, he hadn't come in here to brag, and he *sure* hadn't come to get into a brawl with Denise Trumaine's dang brother.

He kept his mouth shut and carefully took the smile off his face.

"I'm glad I run into you, Halstad," Derek said. "Saves me the trouble of having to look you up."

"Mm?"

"You stay the hell away from my sister. You hear? I won't have no damn farmer sniffing around her. You hear me?"

Billy Ray cocked his head to the side and debated how best he should answer that.

The problem was that he really couldn't make any quick and easy disclaimers to Derek. Not after all the long-night thoughts Billy Ray'd had last night, all of them one way or another centered on this fellow's sister.

He wasn't going to lie, dang it. This hot-tempered youngster was not going to push him into that.

But he didn't want to . . .

"You *hear* me?" Derek snapped.

"Oh, I heard you just fine, thank you."

"Damned farmer."

"Preacher, actually," Billy Ray corrected mildly.

"Damned farmer," Derek repeated. He tilted his chin back and gave Billy Ray a snooty look. The young cowboy's fists relaxed, and he snorted loudly. "You stay away from her, mister, or I'm gonna whip all over you."

Might not be so easy as you think, bub, Billy Ray thought. But he kept it inside and hoped he'd managed to keep it from showing too.

Derek gave him another nasty, glowering look, then turned and stomped outside.

He yanked his horse's reins off the hitch pole and flung himself angrily into the saddle. He wheeled the horse back around toward the west and spurred it hard into a run.

"Sorry about that," Billy Ray said softly.

Mr. Ayres didn't answer. He had gone back to examining his fingernails, which surely by this point couldn't have stood any more trimming or the man would have drawn blood.

Billy Ray shrugged and went back outside into the fading twilight. It was probably time for Mr. Ayres to close up shop anyhow.

20

This mud and mortar business stepped right along once a fellow got the hang of it, Billy Ray reflected with considerable satisfaction.

The west wall was completed now, and nearly half the south-facing front wall too.

He glanced toward the western sky and decided he had time for one more small mix of mortar. He should be able to finish the area above the front door before he called it quits for the night. He jumped down off the piled crates he was using in lieu of a step-ladder, picked up his bucket and hiked down toward the river.

He was pleased. Just these few days and already his muscles were beginning to feel loose and good from the using, instead of aching and paining him all the time. Last night he'd even been able to sleep better, and he woke up today wanting to get on the job quick as he could.

It had been, he decided, just too dang long since he'd done any real work.

He walked with a quick, light, long-striding step, the bucket swinging in time to his pace, and he felt so good all of a sudden that he reared back and began to sing, belting out "Bringing in the Sheaves" near as loud as he could, and altering his gait slightly so his walking and the swinging of the bucket matched the tempo of the hymn.

He reached the line of cottonwoods and marched into their shade to the mortar sump he'd made there.

"Bringing in the sheaves, bring-ing in thu-uh sheaves . . ."

He set the bucket down and turned toward the dirt pit. And clamped his mouth tight shut, a flush of quick embarrassment coloring his face dark and bringing heat to his ears.

"Oh."

Denise laughed and stepped out of the brush. There wasn't any sign of the horse today or he might have noticed her before.

"I'm, uh, sorry," he stammered.

"Don't be. You have a nice voice, Just Billy Ray."

"I don't think I've ever been accused of that before."

"Well it is when you turn loose of it like that. Really."

"Thank you. I suppose."

"Am I interrupting anything?"

He shook his head. No one, probably including the Lord, cared much when — or maybe if — he finished chinking the church walls.

"You're sure?"

"Sure I'm sure."

She helped herself to a seat on a fallen, rotting log and fluffed her riding skirt modestly over her limbs.

"Are you sure you're allowed to be here?" he said.

"Why ever would you ask a thing like that?"

"Mm, I just thought your family might have some objection. Or something."

She sniffed. "Papa doesn't mind what I do. He's a growly old honey-bear, but he's *much* more honey than bear. And I certainly don't care what my brother thinks. He's about the *last* person in the world I'd listen to." She cocked her head prettily to the side and pondered. "Has somebody said something to you?"

"Just kind of an impression I got." Which failed to specify precisely how he'd *gotten* that impression, but certainly fell short of being a lie.

"Oh." She leaned down and picked a fallen leaf off the ground and began studiously concentrating on folding it into tiny accordion pleats.

Billy Ray picked up his shirt and slipped it on for modesty's sake, then squatted on the ground where he could look at her without being too close. My, but she was one awfully pretty girl. No wonder that Derek was wanting to look out for her. Probably the Trumaine household drew single fellows like a picnic draws ants.

"Was there something in particular you wanted to talk to me about?" If she wanted to talk to a preacher about getting married to some pimple-faced, sweat-smelling cowboy he wasn't going to like it, but he did want to know.

"Oh, I don't know. What can you talk about, Just Billy Ray?"

He grinned. His mood had been a good one already, and was especially so now that Denise had shown up. He felt lighthearted and slightly silly. He held one hand up so he could tick things off on his fingers. "Let's see now. I mean, I can't give you an exact answer yet 'cause it isn't exactly a subject I've thought on before. But I could talk to you about birthings and buryings, christenings and cakewalks, marrying, heaven, hell, salvation and baptism, hymns . . . but not much about hers . . . mines and

109

mining, Saturday nights and Sunday mornings . . . whew, there's more here than I'd
expected . . . reading and ciphering, how
deep snow gets in the wintertime, how high
clouds float over the mountains, the color of
an evening sky . . ." He grinned. "Want me
to keep going?"

Denise laughed. "Hold the rest of them in
reserve for a while. Surely we can find something to talk about off that list already."

"Then I hope you remember them all,
'cause I surely don't."

"We'll start at the beginning then," she
said. "Do you have a girlfriend?"

"Funny, I don't at all remember that
being one of the things I mentioned."

"Of course you did. It was the first thing
you said."

"All right, if you say so. No, I don't have
any, um, lady friends."

"Oh my, Just Billy Ray. There's something in your face when you say that . . . You
did have a girlfriend, didn't you?"

He shrugged.

"Be honest now."

"It isn't something I particularly want to
recall."

"Oh dear. I *am* sorry. I truly didn't mean
to bring up anything painful." Her expression was one of genuine concern now.

110

Billy Ray shrugged again. But he didn't want to talk about it. And it *was* painful, darn it.

He'd thought he really reached that girl. Thought there was something kind of nice between them. Her name had been Hattie. And, he admitted it now, he'd been sweet on her in spite of what she'd done for a living. He'd thought she would give all that up and come into the fold. But she hadn't. He'd failed her, was what it came down to.

He had gone and failed Hattie, and he supposed that was about the time he'd started feeling like he was just going through the motions of things, instead of being the proper preacher that folks wanted and expected and truly needed. Truly deserved.

And no, he definitely did not want to sit here and talk to Denise Trumaine about that moldy old history.

Definitely not.

"All right then," Denise said with forced cheerfulness. "We'll go to the second item on your list. Tell me everything you know, please, about cabbages."

"Ah," Billy Ray said solemnly, nodding. "Cabbages are among my favorite topics to discuss, yes."

Denise clapped her hands happily and

111

leaned forward, her eyes sparkling.

She delighted in nonsense as well as in seriousness, Billy Ray realized with pleasure.

He paused only a moment, then launched into a long and complex and entirely imaginary spiel about the growth habits and nutritional values of cabbages, and Denise, giggling, egged him on with frequent comments and questions and additions to his story.

Anyone listening to their silliness might have taken it all to be serious. But only if the listener was unable to see the bright twinkling in her eyes. Which were, he noticed now, a blue as bright and clear as a mountain sky.

So much for being able to sleep comfortably tonight.

Not that he minded.

They talked — about cabbages and horse collars and other weighty matters of the world — until it was dusk and much too late for Billy Ray to get any more work done. Then Denise jumped up from her log with a giggle and a good-bye, and disappeared into the brush as abruptly as she had come.

A moment later Billy Ray heard the staccato thudding of her horse's hooves breaking into a lope.

He grinned.

She'd had the horse hidden away all along. She'd quite deliberately intended to surprise him like that.

The girl, he decided, was as odd as she was pretty. Considerable, on both counts.

21

Much as he would have looked forward to another surprise visit, Denise didn't show up again anytime the rest of the week. Billy Ray minded that but tried not to.

He tried to concentrate instead on the work he was doing, and by early Saturday it was all done, at least all the chinking and caulking that he could get to without climbing onto the roof.

Every wall was fresh-mortared and wind-tight, and he'd even taken some of the clay and touched up the inside of the walls to match the nice, smooth outside. Except for the roof still being so patchy, it looked just fine now, and no one passing by could mistake it for a derelict waiting its turn to fall down.

"Just in time," he said aloud.

This talking to himself out loud was something he'd been doing the past day or so, and he hoped it wasn't going to become a habit.

It hadn't seemed such a bad habit back when his out-loud musing had been prayers, but here lately he hadn't been praying when he was talking alone like that. He was just talking.

"Sorry," he mumbled. But that didn't seem like a prayer either. He sighed and reminded himself to shut up.

He took his bucket back down to the river and cleaned it out, and while he was there he bathed in the cold water and washed off his second-best clothes as well as he could. He had to do that laundry while he was still wearing them, of course, as he didn't have much in the way of spares to change into, but this time of year that was no problem. It was still warm enough that they could dry on him and not be a bother. Come winter it would be another matter entirely.

He slicked his hair back, then picked up the tools he'd fashioned out of the dump leavings and carried them all back to the dugout.

Purgatory City was hopping today, he saw across the barren stretch of field that separated him from the town.

There were people streaming in for their Saturday shopping. Light wagons and saddle horses and a number of kids running around underfoot. It occurred to him that he had no idea where the children around here went to school. There had to be one someplace but he hadn't seen sign of it in the town anywhere, and there weren't any children on the street that he could see through the week. Apparently the school-house was set off by itself like the church was.

Billy Ray pulled a wood chunk around in front of the dugout and upended it so he could sit in the sunshine and dry off. He had a good view of the town from that vantage point.

The folks he could see on the street this Saturday looked to be a prosperous crowd. They were dressed nice, and their driving rigs were mostly light and fairly fancy. They weren't being pulled by any rough, sloggy old cobs either, but by high-stepping harness horses with long lines and small bones.

Billy Ray didn't know much about horses, which was perhaps why they fascinated him. Back home he'd been exposed to the usual drafters and mules and such, and things had been no different in the mining country. Up in the mountains where the gold camps were, a man had no use for a light horse. Anything you needed to reach you could walk to, and hay or grain to feed a useless saddle horse had to be hauled in. Up there the cost to feed a horse would outstrip the worth of the horse in a month or so, so nobody Billy Ray had ever known kept one.

Down here he could see how such an animal would be useful. Here things were spread out more, so that it was a problem getting from one place to the next. And here the cost of feeding wouldn't be anything more than the trouble of putting up a fence or staking the animal out here and there so it could reach the fresh grass that grew everywhere you looked.

He had to admit too that he admired the proud look of them as they trotted by, the saddle horses and the harness stock too. Both were unlike the huge, slow, patient draft animals that drew the freight rigs he was used to.

Come to think of it, he realized, the stock he'd seen last Sunday when his congregation came in were all pretty much like what he was used to. Big and sturdy and powerful. They weren't anything at all like what he was seeing now.

Interesting, he thought.

But only mildly so.

"Really now, you *got* to pay attention to business," he told himself before he realized he'd gone and said it out loud again.

He groaned, disappointed that he'd forgotten his resolution so quickly.

But of course he'd been perfectly right in what he'd said.

He really did have to start paying attention to business.

Tomorrow morning early he had to preach a sermon again, and he hadn't yet given the first thought to what he ought to say.

He quit his woolgathering and went inside to get his Bible. The very least he could do, he figured, was bring the Bible out to read so he could be accomplishing something while he sat in the sun and dried.

22

There was no doubt about it. It was the poorest dang sermon he'd ever given. Bar none. Even that first scared, halting, nervous talk he'd given to a handful of townspeople in Blue Gorge had been better than this.

No, darn it, to be perfectly honest, *especially* that first talk had been better than this one.

At least that time his heart had been in it, even if he didn't know what he was doing.

This morning he'd felt like he was sleep-walking or something.

He went through motions. His mouth worked. Sounds came out. That was about the best thing he could think of to say for himself this Sunday morning.

Oh, yes. His mouth worked *and* he showed up on time.

Thank you very much.

He walked down the aisle to the front door and waited, wondering what these poor, long-suffering folks were thinking of their new dang preacher by now.

They were, well, polite.

They filed out and shook his hand and most of them smiled or mumbled something.

"The hundred-thirteenth psalm for next week, Reverend?" Ad Smits asked dryly.

Billy Ray didn't think the dour-faced farmer was teasing him. But he wasn't positive about that. The main reason he didn't believe it was because he didn't think Smits had a sense of humor. Other than that, Billy Ray would have been almost sure he was teasing.

This morning Billy Ray had talked, sort of, out of the hundred-twelfth psalm, mostly because last week he'd taken the hundred eleventh for his scripture and his marker was already in place on that page.

He'd have done better, he decided now, just to read them some psalms and let it go at that.

He sighed and shook Smits's hand and muttered something that the deacon could take however he wanted.

Heart, he was thinking.

He'd thought it himself, walking down the aisle to the door. Used to be he didn't have so dang much to say, but what there was of it came from his heart.

This morning his heart was stony and silent and dry.

And even in Psalm 112, the very one he'd made such a botch with today, it was talking about heart.

"He shall not be afraid of evil tidings; his heart is fixed, trusting in the Lord."

Seventh verse. Right there in black and white. Today he'd read those words out loud. But he hadn't listened to them.

He wondered if anybody else had listened to them either. He couldn't blame them for not.

"Good day, Reverend," Eli Pieck said softly. "Nice work you've done on the building. We appreciate it."

Billy Ray felt like hugging the man. It wouldn't have been possible for anybody to miss seeing it, but Eli was the only one of them to mention it. At least *some*thing he'd done this week turned out okay.

Of course the other half of Brother Pieck's comment had to do with the failed sermon. That part, mercifully, was left unsaid.

Billy Ray appreciated that too, that Brother Pieck hadn't actually come out and said anything.

He shook a few more hands and thought that these good people really could have done quite as well for themselves if they'd hired in a carpenter instead of a preacher.

That was about the only kind of building-up Billy Ray Halstad seemed able to do for a church lately.

Then again, he reflected, a carpenter would come at a dearer wage than he was being paid here.

And at that they were overpaying him.

He shook the last and final hand and stepped out to the area where the wagons were parked. He wanted to catch Will Elwick before they pulled away. Little Emmy had wanted to ask him something last week, and he hadn't seen her since.

He was too late. Will and his family were already bouncing across the field toward town.

No matter, he decided. He could catch them there.

He passed out the obligatory if perfunctory nods and smiles and comments about the weather, and helped the Krohn boy — Jerry, he recalled after a moment's thought — wrestle a bit into the mouth of a hot and bored and mulishly stubborn mule hitched to their wagon. Mulish. An entirely apt expression, actually. And just when the bit was finally established where it was supposed to be, and Jerry was climbing into the back of the wagon behind his parents, the

122

dang-fool creature blew snot all over the front of Billy Ray's best and only suit coat.

But then it was that kind of day.

He gave the Krohns a smile he didn't feel and waved them off toward town, then followed on foot with the intention of catching up with Emmy and perhaps talking to the child while her folks were doing their shopping.

23

He swung by the dugout on his way toward town. The mule had left his coat in more of a mess than he wanted to be seen in, so he took a few moments to find a scrap of rag and scrub off the front of the coat with a moistened end of the cloth, then hurried along behind the crowd of farmers that had already descended on Purgatory City.

The detour brought him into town from a different angle, so he could see across behind the business buildings and few homes of Purgatory City to the slop joint over on the west end.

Billy Ray had to chuckle to himself in spite of what he happened to see.

There wasn't any sight of the Krohn wagon, it being somewhere on the street and out of view behind the buildings.

But he could see Jerry all right.

The boy was man-sized across the shoulders, if not necessarily so between the ears.

And it looked like young Jerry was feeling

some of the stirrings that came with growing up.

Billy Ray could remember those all right. He just wished now that a fella outgrew all of them, and not just some.

Jerry had come out of a narrow alley that ran between two of the stores, and was cutting through somebody's backyard, throwing frequent peeks over his shoulder and acting like a thief fixing to be caught in the act from his own ineptitude.

It was pretty plain where the boy was headed. He disappeared out of sight behind a shed, reappeared two houses over and then broke into a trot across the open ground between the last houses on that end of town and the saloon. Jerry kept shooting glances over his shoulder lest his father see where he was going and stop him.

The display was more funny than anything else, Billy Ray thought.

What Jerry was up to here was something every boy goes through one time or another.

On the other hand, what Jerry was up to here — or was up to *trying* to do here — was also a sin, and no two ways about it.

Billy Ray changed his direction, heading not toward Mr. Ayres's store now, but across toward the saloon.

He wasn't really sure the lesson Jerry

needed right now was the one he was fixing to get. But the fact was that as Jerry's preacher he was pretty much obligated to remind the boy about what was sinful and what wasn't. Whether Jerry appreciated the lesson or not.

Billy Ray chuckled out loud while he could — once he got to the saloon he'd have to be long-faced and serious, so he could put a thoroughgoing scare into young Jerry — and lengthened his stride to a brisk, positive pace.

24

Jerry Krohn might have gone into the slop joint looking for a good time. But Billy Ray didn't think he was finding one.

By the time Billy Ray walked inside, Jerry was already surrounded by a group of laughing cowboys. There were four of them. They had him ringed inside a narrow circle and were taunting him with language that probably should have made a preacher blush. Most of the jibes were directed at Jerry's clothing. The cowboys — cowhands, darn it — kept telling the boy he stank of pig and chicken manure. Hardly original thinking, Billy Ray thought with amusement. But then the cowhands weren't much older or more worldly-wise than Jerry was. Their experiences were different from Jerry's but not necessarily more illuminating.

Billy Ray crossed his arms over his chest and leaned against the door jamb, giving the bunch of youngsters time to work it out themselves, if they wanted.

"This here place is for men, boy," declared a cowhand who wasn't yet old enough to shave regularly.

"Why lookee here, boys. The clodstomper's wearin' shoes today," another taunted.

"Your papa know you borryed the family's pair o' shoes, boy?"

"Not very nice o' you, boy, makin' your sister go barefoot on Sunday."

Jerry — Billy Ray had to give him credit — tried to ignore the teasing. He took a look around and, finding no painted ladies in the allegedly evil place of business — Shee-oot, Billy Ray thought, any working girl would be hard asleep at this hour of a Sunday afternoon — stepped up to the bar and plunked a coin down.

"Whiskey," he ordered.

The bartender ignored the request.

"No damned farmer's gonna drink in here," one of the cowboys said with loud fervor.

"Whiskey," Jerry repeated stubbornly. He pushed his coin forward.

The cowboys closed in tighter around him, jostling him from both sides. Young Jerry stood half a head taller than the largest of his tormentors, Billy Ray noticed.

"We're done playing with you, farmer boy. Now get the hell outa here." The one who said it grabbed Jerry by the arm and tried to haul him away from the bar.

Jerry sulled up like one of his daddy's mules. He humped his shoulders and yanked his arm free, the force of it driving his elbow backward into the chest of the cowboy behind him. And that right there was enough to put a start on things.

Within seconds the floor in front of the bar was a scramble of fists, feet and elbows, as the four cowboys and then two more who had been watching from the side swarmed onto Jerry Krohn.

Jerry was big enough, but he was neither quick nor experienced. Almost immediately he was streaming blood from his nose and mouth, and a cut had opened over his left eye.

"Hold it," Billy Ray roared.

He stepped forward, picked the nearest cowboy up — a small one — and set him aside.

The cowboys stopped and glared at him. He doubted that any of them had noticed him come inside behind Jerry. Jerry quit trying to fight too.

"Shame on you," Billy Ray told them all. "The whole darn bunch of you ganging up

129

on one boy. Are you cowhands so puny it takes all of you to wale on one farmer kid?" He didn't think an appeal to sweet reason would get him very far here. But a little sting to the cowboys' pride just might.

The young men — the oldest of them didn't look to be much more than twenty — glanced at each other. One of them tilted his head and gave Billy Ray a looking-over.

"You're the damn preacher, ain't you?"

"I'm the preacher, yes. And the whole point of that is that I'm *not* damned." Billy Ray smiled at him.

"An' I am? Is that what you're saying?"

Billy Ray's smile got wider. "You tell me. Are you?"

"You aren't wanted here, preacher. This isn't exactly a good place for the likes of you."

"It kinda strikes me, boys, that it isn't the right kind of place of any of you neither. But that's beside the point, isn't it?"

"We were just . . ."

"Oh, I saw what you were just doing. At six-to-one odds." He looked at Jerry, who was mopping the blood off his face with a handkerchief and carefully avoiding Billy Ray's eyes. "Having fun yet, Jerry?"

The boy didn't answer.

Billy Ray shoved into the middle of them

to stand beside Jerry. He picked up the dime from the bar and tucked it carefully into Jerry's shirt pocket. "I don't think this would be a good day for you to learn how to drink, Jerry. But if you like I can teach you a few things about it." He took Jerry by the shoulders and turned him toward the door. "Go on. Your folks will be looking for you if you don't hurry. You wouldn't want them to find you here."

Jerry gave Billy Ray a brief, guilty look.

"Go get cleaned up, son. I won't tell anybody where you got into your fuss."

The big youngster grinned and bobbed his head. He gave the cowboys a worried look, but they stepped aside to let him through and he headed for the door in a hurry.

"I suppose now you're gonna preach to us 'bout the evils of strong drink. An' other things," one of the cowboys challenged.

Billy Ray grinned. He put his back to the bar and leaned both elbows onto it, his right heel automatically reaching back to hook over the bar rail. It was an old habit that came back to him all too naturally for comfort.

"I hadn't planned on it," he said. "But I'd be happy to if you want to listen."

"What would a damn sky pilot know about fun?"

Billy Ray laughed. "More than you think, as a matter of fact. You think I was always a preacher?" He shook his head. "Used to be a hard-rock miner. You boys know anything about a mining camp on a Saturday night? Well let me tell you, you don't know much about hell-raising 'til you do. So I know what that's like. The point is, I know what the other is like too. You boys only know half the story. I got the whole picture. And believe me, it's even more fun being saved than it is being drunk. I know because I've tried both." He chuckled. "No hangover from being saved. And it makes you jump and shout even better. Makes you feel that dang good."

"Bull."

"No, but I don't expect you to take my word for it. Maybe you'll try it sometime yourself. Then you'll know."

"Bull," the cowboy repeated with conviction.

Billy Ray shrugged. "Suit yourself. I should've known, of course. Anybody too scared to take on a farmer kid at less than six to one would be too scared of being wrong to sit through a church service." He straightened out of his bar-side slouch and touched the brim of his cap. "See you, boys."

He went back outside and tried to find Emmy Elwick, but the detour to the saloon had taken too much time. Her father's wagon was already rolling out the east end of Purgatory City as Billy Ray reached the west side. The farmers in Billy Ray's congregation sure didn't waste much time jawing on their Sunday afternoon visits to the stores.

25

He washed up the pot and single spoon he'd used to make his supper of boiled rice — convenient, cheap, one pot, one spoon, not much mess, not much flavor either but that hardly seemed important — and stretched out on the cot without bothering to light a lamp.

Billy Ray felt . . . lethargic? Sort of. But that was really only the half of it. Useless. That came a little closer. Depressed, certainly. And troubled because he knew he hadn't said anything to those cowboys — cowhands — this afternoon that would really and truly touch them.

Words weren't anything close to enough. Words had to have the fire of conviction behind them to carry feelings with them from one person to another.

Billy Ray felt like he had no fire left in him.

He really would have done better this morning just to read to the congregation.

He was talking to them. But he wasn't *touching* them.

Just like with those cowboys this afternoon.

"I could use some help," he said out loud.

But he didn't have the feeling that anybody was listening.

He closed his eyes, but that was no good. It was barely coming dusk outside. Much too early to try and go to sleep.

Besides, what he was really wanting to sleep for now, he knew, was escape, not rest.

A man can't hardly sleep the rest of his life away.

And a preacher, darn it, was just another man. Just another man who could be as confused as the next guy.

Billy Ray'd had the calling to preach. He *knew* that.

Now he'd gone and lost it.

And he hadn't even known that such a thing was possible.

He'd thought that once called, always found.

Except it wasn't so. It just plain wasn't so.

He twisted over onto his side and tried to believe that he was sleepy. He slowed his breathing and willed himself to sleep. He rolled over and tried the other side. After a few minutes he sat up, quitting the struggle,

135

and walked outside.

It was nearly full dark out, and the air was cool. Off to his right there were some lights showing in the houses. The main street was dark and quiet. There probably was life and noise and movement up at the saloon on the far end of town. That didn't seem fair somehow.

But then fair wasn't what it was all about, was it?

Billy Ray shook his head angrily at himself and stretched his legs into a walk. Walking might help tire him a little and let him get to sleep early tonight.

He headed by force of habit down to the river where the huge, brittle cottonwoods hung over the bank. He followed the slight path his own feet had worn through the brush this week past, and stood beside the remains of his mortar sump.

There was not yet moon or starlight to put a gleam onto the ripples and the eddies in the slow, silent water, so the river surface was a bolt of black velvet in the darkness. Billy Ray stood near it for a time, head down and hands in his pockets. There was no breeze tonight, not even the sound of wind rustling leaves overhead to keep him company. He was aware of the quiet power of the river without being able to hear it.

He tipped his head back, raising his face to the distant sky.

"Oh, God!" he cried out.

Without consciously deciding to do so he found himself on his knees in the moist earth beside the Purgatory.

He clasped his hands and tried to pray.

Words came. But in his heart Billy Ray felt empty.

26

Monday morning was better, if only because the prospect of having work to do gave him something to occupy himself with.

The walls were repaired now, but the biggest part of the chore remained, if he wanted to have the church in shape before winter set in. That dang roof.

Billy Ray stared and fumed and walked around and around the old church building with his thumbs hooked behind his waistband and a scowl on his face.

There wasn't any help for it, though. He wasn't going to get the thing fixed by standing on the ground and glaring at it.

He did have a pretty good excuse for not getting anything done, if he wanted to take it.

He hadn't either the tools nor the materials to put a new roof on the saggy old rafters.

All in all a pretty good excuse, he thought.

Then he sighed. Excuse was exactly what

it was. And he didn't think the Lord would accept excuses. Reasons maybe, but not excuses.

"Are You gonna at least help me with this job?" he asked.

After a moment he added, "Not very talkative this morning, are You? Oh, well. Give me a hand and we'll see can we work it out."

Oddly enough, he did feel a little better after that.

He took a few more laps around the church at ground level without getting any particular inspiration, then wandered over to the town dump to see what he might be able to scavenge in the way of the tools and materials he was lacking.

He took a few laps around that too, with his hands in his pockets and still with the scowl.

The prospects were not exactly promising at first glance.

A hammer and keg of nails and a few dozen bundles of new, freshly cut shingles would have been real nice. Or maybe some sheets of new zinc-coated roofing tin.

Unfortunately nobody in Purgatory City seemed to've been burdened with a surplus of such things lately.

About all that was in ready supply, in fact, were busted crates — the slats and end boards much too small and much too shattered to serve as shingles — and busted glass bottles and discarded tin cans. Apparently because Purgatory City was so far from the centers of commerce and transportation, an awful lot of the fancier food items had to be shipped here preserved in tin cans. Even in Blue Gorge, way back in the mountains, there had been enough regular freight traffic that fruits and vegetables could be had mostly fresh, but not here. Here it seemed if a woman wanted on her table some peaches or tomatoes or even something as common as pork and beans, they had to be bought canned and hauled in. A good half of the trash pile seemed to be made up of discarded tin cans, in one degree of rust or another.

Billy Ray sighed. What the heck could you do with a tin can that . . .

He blinked. Then smiled.

He stepped over to the edge of the trash heap and picked up a reasonably rust-free can and looked it over.

Why not? Just why the heck not.

He dropped the thing onto the hard, sunbaked earth and stomped it flat.

The can squished down to a two-layered bit of hard, smooth, flattened steel that was about the size of a grown man's hand, a hand held with the fingers splayed out a bit; call it a tad over palm-sized.

Billy Ray peered first at the flattened tin can and then over to the nearly roofless church.

Now just why the heck not?

A flat piece of steel like that — for that was what it was now, and not a can any longer — could sure be thought of as a little bitty shingle, now couldn't it.

And what better than a steel roof to turn snow and water and wind.

A steel roof would rust. But in a dry climate like this it would take years for that to be a problem. And it wasn't like replacement shingles would be a big expense or anything. He could see for himself how long tin cans lasted in this climate. Judging from what he could see underfoot, they lasted next to forever.

Billy Ray began to grin.

Why not. Tack flattened tin cans all over the roof, start at the bottom and give them a little overlap one can to the next . . . why all a fella had to do was do that often enough — it would take a world of them, true — and by and by he'd have a whole new roof in place.

"Ha!" He tipped his head back and hollered, "Thanks, Boss."

He rubbed his palms together, still grinning, "I still need nails, You know."

He picked up one of the many broken crates in the dump. There were heaps of them, the accumulation of years.

Wood crates are nailed together, he noticed. Every one of the busted crates held several dozen tacks and brads and small, cheap nails of one description or another.

A guy could pull all those nails . . . no, better yet, a guy could have himself a bonfire. Clear a nice, smooth stretch of hardpack and burn the broken crates, then sift the ash and what would he have left? Why, nails of course. Nails and brads and tacks and staples and whatever else somebody somewhere had once used to hold bits of wood together into a crate shape.

"Thanks," he yelped again loudly. "Got a nice new hammer for me, Boss?"

That proved a bit harder. And he should have known better than to get greedy and ask for a *new* hammer.

Which didn't mean that the Boss wasn't still on the job this morning.

After some kicking around through the dump, he found what was left of a broken framing hatchet. The blade part of the hatchet had been shattered so that the upper corner of it was broken clean away. What was left wouldn't do anybody any

142

good for cutting. But the hammerlike balance knob on the other side of it was still just fine. Even the handle was in pretty good shape. A little soaking to swell the wood, and some pounding with a rock to reset the wedges, and the thing would make a jimdandy hammer.

"Ha!" Billy Ray shouted again. "Thank You kindly."

He picked up his new hammer, grinning, and pondered the question now of how he ought to go about turning probably a couple thousand old tin cans into that many tiny shingles.

That, he realized, would take only time and a little effort.

"Hoo-whee. Thank You kindly."

27

Billy Ray sat spraddle-legged on the ground, with the sawed-off tree trunk section he'd been using for a stool standing upright between his extended legs.

He reached over to his left and picked up one of the tin cans he'd gleaned from the dump, set it on top of the flat surface of the wood chunk, picked up a river-slick rock that weighed four pounds or so and had been plucked out of the Purgatory, and whacked the tin can a few good ones.

Presto, he had another shingle.

He took the new shingle and pitched it to his right to join the others, then reached for another can.

This was going all right, by golly.

He could make five, six shingles a minute at this rate, and was getting quicker at it as the work became habit. The only real holdup was having to get up and gather more tin cans every now and then.

Over by the dugout the former hatchet,

now hammer, was soaking head-down in a bucket of river water. Tonight or tomorrow, he figured, he could set the wedges in it and be ready for serious business.

He still had to have his bonfire to collect the nails for the job. But that too was only going to be a matter of time, and not nuisance.

He didn't really have to be in any huge hurry. He simply had to get it done.

Billy Ray grinned and reached for another tin can that was fixing to become a shingle.

Lay it in place, whack with the river rock, reach for another can. You bet.

28

Billy Ray stood, stretching over backward and windmilling his arms to ease the kinks in his lower back and shoulders. It was positively amazing how painful a new activity could be when you repeated it a whole day long. But he had a nice pile of tin shingles already. Why, a few thousand more and he might have enough to start working with.

His bucket was still in use, the broken hatchet standing in it upside-down to swell the wood fibers in the handle, so he had to walk down to the river to wash.

At least this job wasn't as dirty as the mud had been. He could get away with a little washing up and not have to take a whole bath. Late as he'd worked today, the air was already becoming chill, and it would have been uncomfortable getting wet all over.

He began to smile once he was inside the line of cottonwoods.

This evening he could see Denise's horse tied in plain sight.

"Hello, Just Billy Ray." She was seated on the same fallen log she had used before.

"Miss Trumaine." He touched the bill of his cap.

"My, aren't we formal today, Mr. Halstad." He grinned.

"Join me?" She patted the log beside her.

"Only if I can have the downwind side."

Denise laughed. But she also scooted over sideways so there was room for him on the other side.

Billy Ray was struck all over again by how pretty she was. He sat nearby, very much aware that he had been working in the hot sun all the day long and hadn't washed yet. He was careful to avoid getting too close to her.

"I was hoping you would come down to the river tonight," she admitted, bringing a flush of quick pleasure to his cheeks and an accelerated pace to his heartbeat.

"Anytime you want to visit, I mean if you want to talk or anything, you can come by the church, you know. I mean, that is what I'm there for." He smiled. "Even if nobody seems to have gotten the hang of that yet."

Denise shot a look through the trees and the undergrowth toward the bench of open ground where the church and the dugout sat. It was, he thought, a rather solemn, almost troubled look.

"Did I say something wrong?"

She shook her head quickly. He wasn't sure that he believed the denial.

"So what were you wanting to talk about, Miss Trumaine?"

She glanced quickly back toward him, as if questioning whether he was being serious about the return to a formal address. He was smiling. Her expression softened, and she smiled again too.

"I like you, Just Billy Ray."

"Thank you. I like you too."

"No, I mean . . . you don't think I'm just a flibbertigibbet."

"Of course not. You aren't a . . ." he grinned, ". . . one of those whatchamacall-its."

"Papa thinks I am. Derek thinks I am."

He shrugged. "That doesn't make it so."

"See? I knew there was a reason why I liked you, Just Billy Ray."

"Yes, well, I did wonder, of course." He gave her a rueful smile. "I'm certainly glad somebody around here does." He thought, but didn't say, that Denise seemed to be the only one in or around Purgatory City who did.

"Could I ask you something?"

"Certainly."

"What is it, I mean what is it exactly, that a preacher *does?*"

"Well, there is always the obvious. He preaches."

"What about?"

"You really don't know." It wasn't a question.

"No, I really don't."

"It's kind of funny that I should be surprised by that question. It's an honest question and a good one. And it's one I might have asked myself just a few years ago. Now . . . I don't know, Denise . . . habit, I guess. I've gotten into habits that I didn't used to have. So now it surprises me when somebody . . . you, that is . . . asks me a perfectly honest, perfectly valid question." He paused for a moment to give her question some thought.

"The simplest answer, Miss Trumaine, is that a preacher preaches . . . teaches, really . . . about God."

"I've always heard about God," she said. "But mostly just the word. And to be perfectly honest . . . I hope this won't shock you . . . mostly I suppose I've heard the word used in connection with bad language. When the hands don't know I'm close enough to overhear. But I couldn't say that I know anything about God."

"That's an easy problem to solve. The whole idea of being a preacher is telling people about God."

Billy Ray blinked.

That was true, wasn't it?

That *was* the whole idea of being a preacher.

But it wasn't really what he'd been doing here in Purgatory City.

Maybe, like just once in a great while, maybe sometimes Billy Ray Halstad ought to listen to himself when he said something.

Like this evening, for instance.

He grimaced. This Sunday morning past, last Sunday morning before it, he'd worked on sermons that came from the Bible, sure, but they weren't so much telling people plain and simple about God as they were rephrasing the words in the Bible. He wasn't preaching God, he was preaching the Bible. And there was a difference.

Huh. That one he was going to have to think over some.

He turned back to Denise. "Sorry. I was woolgathering for a minute there. You, uh, got me to thinking about something."

"Something good, I hope."

"Yeah." He grinned. "Yeah, I think so."

"I'm glad, then."

"Look, do you want me to tell you about God?"

"Would you mind?"

"Mind? I'd be delighted to."

Denise nodded and folded her hands primly in her lap. "All right, teacher. I'm ready if you are."

29

Billy Ray brushed his hands off and turned toward the west to decide how much daylight he had left.

If he started the bonfire this afternoon he would have to stay until the fire died down — he certainly didn't want to chance starting a grass fire; that would be no way to endear himself to his neighbors — and there really wasn't enough time left to do that and meet Denise too.

Not that he was sure she would be able to make it this evening.

She hadn't been able to come on Wednesday or again yesterday, but she had told him to begin with that she couldn't be away from the house every evening. When her father was in one of his moods — whatever that was supposed to mean — she had to stay at home with him.

Billy Ray hoped she could make it this evening. Tomorrow was Saturday, and he would be busy working on his sermon tomorrow evening.

He enjoyed their evening visits more than he would have cared to admit, to Denise or to anyone else. He looked forward to them all day long, and was disappointed if she was not there waiting for him in the cotton-woods when his day's work was finished.

It really would have been much simpler, he thought, if she would agree to come talk to him at the church while he worked on the roofing materials. She had said herself that she was free during the days for the most part, but for some reason she insisted on talking to him by the river.

Not that he was complaining. It was a pleasure being able to talk to her wherever she chose to be. But it was a little puzzling too.

He went over to the dugout to wash up and have a belated lunch. He'd worked through the noon hour, stripping the dump of all the old crates and wood scraps he could find, and dragging them to the area he had cleared for his bonfire.

And near the church walls he already had an entirely respectable pile of small shingles waiting to be put in place.

Very many more and there wouldn't be an empty can left in the entire dump. He hoped he had enough to do the job. If he didn't

. . . well, there would be enough. That was all there was to it. If there weren't enough tin cans, the Boss would give him some other idea that would work just as well.

Billy Ray believed that. Now. He might have been doubtful a week ago, but not today. His talking with Denise Trumaine had probably done a lot more for Billy Ray Halstad than it did for her.

He ate quickly, anxious now to finish and walk down to the river and find out if Denise would be there today.

He didn't even take time to wash the pot he'd cooked his lunch in — he was beginning to feel that he might soon turn into a glob of gluey, starchy rice, but it was the cheapest and most filling thing he could think of — just set the pot and spoon aside to be washed later.

He hurried shamelessly the whole way down to the river and as soon as he got into the cottonwoods began to smile. The horse was there. He knew Denise would be waiting for him on the log.

30

"You seem in an awfully pensive mood this evening."

"Does it show? I'm sorry."

He smiled. "Nothing to be sorry about. Is anything wrong?"

She shook her head.

"Okay, now try and convince me you're telling the truth."

This time Denise smiled. "It's just something silly. Really."

"It isn't at all silly if it's bothering you."

She sighed. "You know, Just Billy Ray, I believe you're the only man I've ever met who would say such a thing. Papa or Derek either one, they'd be so pleased that I didn't want to bother them with a female-type problem that they wouldn't *want* to know what it was. They certainly wouldn't encourage me to talk about it."

"Female prob . . . oh, my." He felt his ears turn hot.

Denise laughed. "Not *that* kind of female

problem. I mean, it isn't anything *physical*."

"In that case, uh . . ." his ears still felt awfully hot.

She laughed again. Her voice was musical and her laughter a joy to hear. He really liked it when Denise laughed. "I've embarrassed you."

"Would you believe me if I denied it?"

"I thought preachers weren't supposed to lie."

"So much for that way out, then." He grinned at her.

Denise reached over and lightly touched the back of his wrist. "See? You've already made me feel ever so much better."

"I did? Mmm, good for me."

"Yes, good for you, indeed."

"So are you going to tell me what it is that's bothering you?"

"Are you sure you want to hear this? Shouldn't we just forget about it and get on with the lesson?"

"The lesson can wait a few minutes."

Denise sighed, serious again now. She turned her head away so that she wasn't looking at him. He waited, but she didn't immediately speak.

"You know," he said, "talking things over and trying to help folks work out their troubles is one of the things I'm supposed to be

156

doing here, even if I don't see anybody often enough to be doing much good that way yet."

He was watching her back. He could see her shoulders move and her back straighten as she took a deep breath. When she finally spoke, her voice was small.

"Tell me, Just Billy Ray, what would you think about a girl who had certain . . . feelings . . . for a gentleman. Even though that gentleman was older and didn't give any indication of . . . returning such feelings. Would you think a girl like that was a hussy?"

He was glad Denise wasn't looking at him.

He was able to keep from making any sound, but what she was saying drove a spike of pain into his chest.

He had "certain feelings" for *her* — there was no sense in trying to deny it, at least not to himself — and now she wanted his advice about how she should go about attracting the attention of a gentleman?

Billy Ray shot a look upward and thought, This one isn't fair, Boss.

Which did nothing to solve the problem. Not hers. Not his own. Didn't make him feel any better either. And it *wasn't* fair.

Billy Ray took a deep breath too. There were things he'd had to do that were more fun than this.

Denise was sitting rigid as a frightened cottontail.

"You being the girl in question?" he asked softly.

She nodded but kept her back to him.

"You are not a hussy," he said, this time his voice firm about it. "It is perfectly normal for a woman and a man . . . I mean . . . it's in God's proper order of things for there to be marriages. God created us. He put those feelings into us. There isn't anything wrong with the feelings, you see. It's what people do with their feelings that can be wrong. Not the feelings themselves. There isn't anything at all wrong about the feelings themselves. We're supposed to have them. They're what leads us to marriage and children and happiness."

"But if the man doesn't have those feelings too . . . ?"

Then he's one dumb . . . He thought it but didn't say it. And only barely stopped himself in time from adding some words of description that he definitely oughtn't.

"How do you know he doesn't?" he countered.

"He's never shown any such feelings."

"Have you ever shown yours?"

"No. But a girl can't. Not without seeming a hussy, can she?"

158

That wasn't a question Billy Ray had ever considered before, neither as a preacher nor as a man.

"I don't know," he admitted. "I realize girls are supposed to be taught to be shy. A girl who is brazen, well, I know what people think about that."

"So I can't really discuss this with . . . the gentleman in question. Can I?"

"Not in so many words, I suppose."

"So what words can I use?"

"Could you ask your mother how she, um, handled the problem? Like when she met your father and was, well . . . ." He coughed into his fist, not sure just how far he ought to take that subject. It was just as well he didn't go any further with it.

"You ask her," Denise said bitterly. "She's dead."

"Oh!"

She spun on the log to face him. "I'm sorry. I shouldn't have said that. You didn't know, did you?"

"No. Of course, I didn't. I wouldn't have . . . Look, I'm the one who's sorry. I didn't know. I certainly didn't mean to cause you any pain."

She touched his wrist for the second time. But this time there was no surge of pleasure in it.

This time, damn it — there, he'd thought it and he wasn't even sorry — she wasn't being lighthearted and happy. And it wasn't for him that she was touching him anyway. Hadn't been before either, of course.

Now, damn it, he knew that she was wanting his counsel about how she was supposed to go about attracting someone else.

This isn't fair, Boss, he thought again.

"I know you didn't," she said. "I guess I'm a little edgy this evening. Will you accept my apology? Please?"

"There isn't any need," he said stiffly, turning his head away to look at the river.

"Please?"

He looked back at her. Lordy, she was the most beautiful girl he would ever in his life see. It hurt now, just looking at her. He forced a smile. "If you'll accept mine."

She nodded solemnly.

"As for the, um, other, uh, situation . . ."

She dropped her eyes.

"I really don't know what to tell you. Would you mind if I think about it before I say something that could be wrong? We could talk about it another time?"

Denise nodded. She too seemed anxious to get that line of conversation behind them now. She was embarrassed, he guessed.

"Would you mind if we skipped to-

160

night's lesson?" she asked.

"Whatever you prefer."

"I think I should get home now. It will be all the way dark soon."

It had been fully dark every other time she had left to return home from her evening rides. He didn't say anything about that. She stood and walked toward her horse, and Billy Ray trailed along unhappily behind her.

"Would you come to church?"

"I don't think I can."

"Of course."

She stopped, looked at him, but she said nothing.

He walked with her to the horse and took her elbow to help her mount. "Tomorrow evening . . . ?"

"Maybe. If I can. Maybe."

He nodded. The lessons were still good ones. The ones she was learning from him and the ones she was teaching him about his own faith by listening to him.

But it wouldn't be at all the same now, he knew.

Now he would just be preaching.

Before . . . Before he'd had ideas that Denise might someday have those feelings about him.

That was the plain and simple truth of it.

He'd been setting himself up with stupid, stupid notions.

It was really his own stupid fault.

She hadn't led him on. Not a bit.

Dumb SOB, Billy Ray silently castigated himself.

"Good night, Billy Ray."

She could feel the difference too, he supposed. She called him Billy Ray and not by the light, friendly Just Billy Ray.

"Good night, Denise."

She reined the horse away through the trees and disappeared into the shadows within seconds.

Billy Ray turned and walked heavily back to the log. He slumped onto it, heartsick and miserable.

"Godspeed, Denise," he whispered.

He raised his eyes and asked, "Why, Lord? Why'd You go and send me here?"

An answer would have been awfully welcome, but the only thing he heard was the soughing of a gentle breeze through the cottonwoods, and a low gurgle from the river.

31

Billy Ray was covered with soot and ash and grime. Salty sweat-tracks streaked white stripes down his sides and bare chest where the running sweat had temporarily washed the soot away.

The day would not have been all that uncomfortably warm, but having to stay so close by the fire was miserably hot.

He was thirsty and hungry from not wanting to leave the bonfire long enough to tend to such needs, and he had to use the outhouse bad.

His mood probably would have been sour except for the fact that he was getting so much accomplished.

It was mid Saturday afternoon and the bonfire was burning down now. He figured he could let it cool through tomorrow — that would give it some time, too, for the wind to help by carrying loose ash away — and then Monday morning he could sift the pile to recover the nails and tacks and brads he needed.

He'd been worried about how to do that but thought he had it worked out now. He'd found a battered kerosene tin in the dump and pried the top off it, then used a bent nail and his hammer to poke holes in the bottom of the tin so that it became like a sieve or colander. Wet ash would flow through the holes in a slurry, but the nails would remain behind. And any bits of wood left would float to the top to be skimmed off when he filled the tin with a mixture of water and ash from his bonfire. He'd gotten the idea from the way the stamp mills worked when they were recovering gold from the mined ore in the mountains.

He stepped further into the ring of intense heat and used a piece of broken wagon tongue, also recovered from the dump, to stir the fire and move the remaining bits into an ever-smaller pile. He wanted the wood to burn as completely as possible so it would leave only the metal and dry ash behind.

A palm-sized scrap of crate slatting flared into bright flame, and Billy Ray smiled.

A puff of breeze lifted ash and glowing embers into the air, and he watched them carefully. He had a bucket of river water handy just in case a grass fire was ignited, but so far he hadn't had to use it.

He was concentrating so hard on what he was doing that he didn't hear the horsemen until they were almost to him. But then he had been hearing horses most of the day, as people came into town for their Saturday shopping and Saturday night celebrating.

There were two of them, he saw when he looked up. Cowboys. Both of them young. He thought he recognized them from last Sunday. He thought they had been among the boys who were teasing Jerry Krohn then.

"Hello." He smiled.

Neither of the cowboys smiled back at him. They pulled their horses to a stop a few yards away and scowled down at him.

"Is there something I can do for you?"

"You can quit trying to burn the town down, for one thing," one of them drawled.

"I'm almost done. I don't think there's been any danger."

"We say there's been plenty danger. You should have better sense."

"Aw, you can't expect sense outa a preacher. 'Specially a farmer preacher."

"We want you to quit this burning. It's dangerous."

"Yes, well, it's about burned down now."

" 'About' ain't good enough. We want you to put it out."

"And I said it's almost out already. There

165

is no fire danger. You can see that for your-selves."

"Put it out."

"No, I don't think I will do that. But I'm sure I thank you for your civic pride and deep concern for your neighbors." He smiled.

"Put it out."

"Huh-uh."

The one who had been doing most of the talking tossed his reins to his friend and dis-mounted. He was tall and lean and young and fit. He flexed his hands into fists and waved his arms around like he was lim-bering up for a contest of strength.

Billy Ray grinned. "You're trying to scare me, right?"

"You better be scared, preacher man. Either you put that fire out your own self or I'll pick you up and drag you through it to put it out."

"You know, sonny, I kind of get the im-pression that if I do what you say, you'll be awfully disappointed. I mean, think about it. If I do exactly what you want, you won't have any excuse to bluster and threaten and bash me around."

"Put the fire out," the cowboy said. He came closer, glowering and scowling.

Billy Ray laughed. "Now you're making

faces. You should see yourself when you do that."

"I'm warning you . . ."

"Oh, come on now. Let's cut to the bottom of this. What is it you're trying to do here?"

"We are trying, polite as we know how, to let you know that we don't want your kind around here."

"My kind? You have something against preachers?"

"You know what I mean."

"I'm sorry, but as it happens, I don't know. I really don't."

"You come in here as some damned farmer preacher an' you encourage those farmers. They get all settled down here an' more of them will come. We don't want them here. We don't want you here."

"Thank you. Now I'm beginning to get the picture. I appreciate that."

"You think I won't hit you just 'cause you're a damned preacher?"

"Didn't we already have this discussion about me not being the one who's damned?"

"You . . ."

"No, sonny . . ."

"Don't you be calling me that again."

"To answer your question. Sonny. No, I

167

don't think you would be afraid to hit me because I'm a preacher. But I think you'd better be afraid to hit me. Because if you do. Sonny. I won't turn my cheek but the one time. You understand me now? The Book only says about turning it the once. I don't remember a single place where it says I have to stand for being beaten up by a couple young idjits." Billy Ray smiled at both of them again and laid the wagon pole down so he wouldn't be tempted to use it. He'd always had something of a temper once he got started, and he didn't want to carry this silliness too far.

The cowboy clouded up and flexed his shoulder muscles.

"Come ahead then, but I suggest you have your buddy climb down and join you." He grinned. "Just to make it fair."

"You stay right where you are, Bobby. I don't need no help with the preacher man here."

"Suit yourself then." Billy Ray turned to face the cowboy and waited for him to throw the first one.

32

The cowboy drew his fist back in slow, deliberate aim.

Billy Ray continued to stand there smiling at him. That was really a terrible thing to do to him, Billy Ray knew. It was taunting him. And probably that was wrong. He would work that out later when he thought about it. Right now he didn't have much time to ponder the question.

The cowboy's fist lashed out in a punch hard enough to do some real damage. He wasn't playing about it. He meant to do some serious hurt.

Billy Ray swayed a few inches to his right, and the fist flashed harmlessly past his ear.

Billy Ray took a step back and turned his face to the side, pointing to his chin. "Okay, I turned it. That's the one free one you're entitled to."

The cowboy bellowed and threw another one.

Billy Ray slipped that punch too, this time

to the other side. "You're starting to annoy me, sonny."

The cowboy gritted his teeth and launched himself straight forward, head down and both arms flailing.

He wasn't really much more adept at fistfighting than Jerry Krohn had been, Billy Ray thought. No wonder those boys had wanted to take the big farmer kid on six at a time.

Billy Ray backpedaled, staying just ahead of the cowboy until he lost his balance and tipped forward too far to right himself.

Billy Ray stopped, gauged the timing carefully and lifted a knee full into the cowboy's face.

The one called Bobby was off his horse by then and joining into the fray.

Too late, though, for his help to make a fair contest of it.

Billy Ray chopped him down like a sapling falling to a double-bitted ax, then got a rag and his bucket and went to cleaning the cowboys up.

He whistled "Swing Low, Sweet Chariot" through his teeth while he washed them off and got them to feeling better.

33

Billy Ray regretted what he'd done practically the first minute after those cowboys crawled back onto their horses and rode toward the saloon at the far end of town.

There really should be a better way than this.

It was a terrible example he was setting, allowing himself to be drawn into a fight.

And an unfair fight, at that.

That was really what made it so bad.

He sighed. At least there was one nice thing he could reflect on.

It was a bad example he would be setting only if there was someone around to set an example *for*.

The truth was that no one in or around Purgatory City seemed to give a particular darn *what* he did.

He brushed his hands off and took another look at the fire to make sure it was dying and there really was no danger that it could spread and cause harm.

Then he looked skyward with a grimace.

"I'm really messing You up around here, aren't I. Sorry."

With a shake of his head he picked up the length of wagon tongue and began poking in the ashes again to make sure the fire burned itself fully out.

As soon as it was safe to leave the fire, he would go back to the dugout and start thinking about tomorrow's sermon.

Although probably it would be more useful if he forgot about that and kept on with his carpenter work instead.

34

Nothing.

Nothing, nothing. NOTHING.

Thank you very much.

Billy Ray left the little study table and crossed the dirt floor of the dugout to throw himself on the bunk with his hands pressed over his eyes and emptiness in his heart.

He had nothing to say to those people tomorrow. Nothing.

He read, but chapter and verse gave him no inspiration.

He prayed, but the sounds were hollow. Mere words without feeling.

He hoped, but the hopes were empty and in vain.

"So what do I do now?" he asked aloud.

He sat upright on the side of the bunk with a long, audible sigh.

Just keep on keeping on, he told himself.

He'd heard Brother Greer say that once. When things get bad, you bow your neck and bow your head and just keep on keeping on. It'd seemed good advice at the time.

Billy Ray wondered how Brother Greer would've handled things here in Purgatory City.

He wished he could have a long talk with Brother Greer now.

Brother Greer was the itinerant tent-preacher who had come to Blue Gorge that time — a long while back, it seemed now — and first opened Billy Ray's eyes to salvation.

It had all seemed so much fun then. Clean and sweet and joyous.

So where in the years since had he lost all of that?

He just didn't know.

He stood, recrossed the room and blew the lamp out. There was no sense in wasting coal oil to no purpose. The interior of the dugout went dark. Billy Ray hadn't realized it was becoming so late. The open door admitted only the pale last traces of twilight from outside.

He drifted outdoors. The evening air was fresh and clean. From off in the direction of town he could hear the distinctive sounds of merriment. The Saturday afternoon shoppers had all gone home by now, and the stores were closing. The town belonged now to the drinkers and the fornicators and the hell-raisers.

Billy Ray stared off toward the distant saloon. But instead of peering toward it with distaste — or even with compassion and a wish for the salvation of those unknowing boys who were dissipating themselves in sin — he looked toward it with something that was painfully akin to a longing.

His mouth watered, and he could practically taste the cool, sharp bite of beer on his tongue.

Worse, he felt a sudden, unwelcome urgency of need deep in his belly.

There would be women over there too. Wicked women. The kind who were willing, in exchange for a coin.

Thirty pieces of silver, he reminded himself.

But knowing that did not make the desires go away.

Billy Ray groaned out loud.

He turned away from the lights and the noises of the town and broke into a run, hoping he could substitute the exhaustion of physical efforts for the body's other demands.

He ran toward the river. And even as he ran, he knew that he was trying to hide an unwelcome truth from himself.

Oh, he was wanting to force himself to exhaustion, all right. That was true enough. But it wasn't all the truth.

The rest of it was that he was quietly, privately, secretively hoping that he would encounter Denise Trumaine somewhere along the Purgatory.

And if he did . . . well . . . he wouldn't. Of course he wouldn't. So there was no need to think about what might happen if he did. Because he wouldn't. But if he did . . .

He shook his head, shuddering, and loped on through the gathering night until his chest ached from want of air to breathe, and his sides hurt and his legs were weak and trembly.

And still he ran as if trying to escape from something.

35

The sermon Billy Ray finally delivered on Sabbath morning had all the fiery conviction of a dictionary being read aloud. And at that it was probably an improvement. He felt sorry for the people in the congregation who were suffering through by having to listen to him.

It just wasn't there. Whatever *it* was.

Inspiration? God? Whatever, whomever, Billy Ray was alone at the pulpit that morning.

He filled most of the service with hymns — which went over much better than his talking — and cut the whole thing as short as he was decently able.

He was able to meet very few eyes as the families passed out the door and offered perfunctory handshakes.

One set of small, trusting eyes he did meet was that of Emmy Elwick. "I've been trying to find you to have that talk you wanted, Emmy. Could we . . ."

The child looked pleased and then, just as quickly, disappointed, as from a few feet away her father angrily called for her. "Come along, Emmy. Hurry. You know we have things to do before we can get back for the choring."

"Yes, Papa." She gave Billy Ray a flashing look of apology and trotted obediently off toward the family wagon.

Perhaps he could still catch her in town while her parents did their Sunday shopping.

Billy Ray continued the routine of handshaking. As usual, the two deacons Eli Pieck and Ad Smits were the last members of the congregation to leave.

"Do you have a minute, Reverend?" Smits demanded in a voice that said it was no question at all. The reverend had *better* have a minute to give to his deacons.

Even Eli looked agitated this morning.

Not that Billy Ray could blame either of the men. They had a right to be angry. Their new preacher was failing them.

Billy Ray sighed.

So it was coming to this. He was going to be fired.

It was one thing to have been fired from a mining job. It was quite another to be fired out of one's calling.

But he really couldn't blame them.

"Would you like to step into the privacy of the church?" he suggested.

It would be a little more bearable, perhaps, if the rest of the congregation was not standing around watching, knowing, eavesdropping.

He suspected the farmers would have talked it over among themselves during the week.

Surely they would have. Wherever they all lived, surely they must see one another through the workweek. They would have had time to discuss their pastor's failings. They would have reached a decision. Now . . .

"That would be fine, Reverend," Smits said sternly. He gave Eli a haughty, triumphant glance and marched into the sanctuary with his chin high.

Brother Pieck seemed not at all haughty about it, but certainly he was firm in his expression.

Billy Ray trailed the two deacons inside.

"There's something we need to talk to you about, Reverend," Smits began.

"Something important," Pieck added.

"Been bothering us, it has."

"Terrible," Eli agreed.

"So we come to you about it," Smits said.

179

Billy Ray nodded. "I understand. I will do as you gentlemen think best."

"Pardon?"

"I said . . ."

"But that's the trouble," Smits interrupted. "We don't know what *is* best."

"Which is why we came to you," Eli explained.

Billy Ray frowned. Did they want him to make this easier for them by volunteering to resign? If that was what they wanted, well, he supposed the decent and proper thing to do would be to oblige them. After all . . .

"It's a question we read different," Eli said.

"It's a question *Eli* reads different," Smits said. "I'm right. I know I am."

"You are *not*," Pieck said with strained patience.

"I am, damn it."

"Ad," Eli cautioned. "Not in the church."

"Sorry."

"We read it differently," Eli said again.

"And I'm right about it," Smits insisted.

This was terrible, Billy Ray thought. Not only had he come in and made a botch of the preaching, now he was dividing the congregation over whether to fire him or not. Really the only right thing to do was to resign now before there was a split in the family of the church.

He opened his mouth to say the words, but neither Brother Pieck nor Brother Smits was listening.

The deacons had begun to argue. And the argument was becoming heated.

The three men were sitting now on the rearmost pew. Billy Ray was squeezed in between the two farmers, his head swiveling back and forth in an attempt to keep up with the growing flow of sharp words and angry retorts.

"Free will," Eli Pieck was snarling.

"Predestination," Ad Smits growled.

"If you read in . . ."

"But it says that . . ."

Billy Ray tried to hide a grin but wasn't all that successful about it.

Was this what all the furor was about?

This old chestnut?

He leaned back and hooked his hands over an upraised knee so he could get his face out of the line of fire. Spittle had begun spraying off fast-moving lips as the two deacons debated a point of theology with more heat than accuracy.

Billy Ray managed to stop himself from laughing, but couldn't contain a chuckle.

"When you're done with your dogfight, gentlemen," he suggested, "we'll discuss this."

36

"Do I have your attention, gentlemen? Are you done scrapping with one another?"

Brother Pieck nodded. Brother Smits did so too, but a trifle sullenly.

Billy Ray smiled. He stood and stepped over the pew bench and sat facing rearward on the next pew. The deacons turned so that they sat facing him.

"Now the way I understand this," Billy Ray said, "you, Eli, believe that God intended man to have free will. Is that right?"

"Absolutely," Eli said. "It says right in the beginning, right in Genesis . . ."

Ad Smits tried to interrupt. Billy Ray stopped both of them. "Hold up there just a second." He looked from one deacon to the other. "You, Ad, you find that the Reverend Mr. Calvin's doctrine of predestination should hold. Is that correct?"

"Of course it's correct. Any man that's ever done any thinking on the subject . . ."

"Hold on there, I told you."

Billy Ray smiled. "As it happens, gentlemen, this question of free will versus predestination is one of the great bugaboos of Protestant doctrine. It vexed me something awful the first I heard of it. And I got to tell you I did some real serious studying on it before I made up my mind. Wrote a lot of letters. Talked to everybody I could make hold still to tell me what they think. And, gentlemen, I do believe I finally worked it out."

Pieck and Smits each gave the other a smug look. Each still believed he was right.

Eli Pieck was convinced beyond doubt that mankind has a God-given right to error and failure, but has the parallel right to choose good over evil.

Ad Smits followed the strict Calvinist doctrine that each man is predestined before birth either to heaven or to hell, and that no conscious decision man can make is capable of changing the destiny God ordained for him before his conception.

The two deacons were poles apart on the centuries-old question.

"You have the answer?" Eli asked.

Ad gave Billy Ray a suspicious look.

"Yup," Billy Ray said easily.

"Well?" Smits demanded.

Billy Ray grinned. He leaned back and spread his hands and with an ingratiating smile said, "You're both right."

The two deacons roared. Smits jumped off the pew with his fists balled. "If you think you're going to set there and make fun of us . . ."

Billy Ray laughed. "Calm down, Ad. Let me explain. And see if I don't make sense."

Smits frowned, but he sat.

"Reverend," Eli said, "you are taking this almighty light. We are trying to be serious here."

"So am I, Eli. Really. You came asking my opinion. Now listen for a minute and let me give it. Like I say, it's something that plagued me for a long while. Took me the better part of two years to work it out. So listen to what I have to say. Please."

Eli grunted. He sat down and glanced toward Ad. If nothing else, Billy Ray thought, he had at least brought the deacons into agreement on one thing. Both of them now were convinced that their preacher was daft.

"One thing I think we can all agree on, gentlemen, is that God is right."

Both men grunted. This wasn't a point they could argue with.

"Man is subject to error. God is not. God is right, whatever any of us chooses to believe. Right?"

"Right," Eli agreed.

"And man has made a royal mess of some things. In particular on this question of free will versus predestination. And I say that because it is man that has said the two concepts *oppose* each other. They don't."

"But . . ."

"Hush, Ad. Let me finish."

Smits settled back down onto the pew. Reluctantly.

"I've read Calvin's doctrine," Billy Ray said. "It makes a lot of sense."

Smits snapped a look at Pieck.

"But so does Wesley," Billy Ray said. "And I've read him too." Ad Smits looked confused, so he added, "He preached the doctrine of salvation by faith rather than by predestination."

Smits grunted. It was Pieck's turn to look smug.

"What I've finally come to conclude," Billy Ray said, "is that the two doctrines honestly are not in opposition. The people who support one view over the other may be. But not the Word."

"I don't understand," Eli Pieck admitted.

"Okay. What I think happened, gentlemen, is that John Calvin a long time ago reached a very thoughtful conclusion. But he doomed the lot of all the rest of us who followed after him, doomed us to confusion, not because of his ideas about the Bible and the Word of God, but because of his choice of one simple word when he was trying to explain his doctrine.

"What I think, gentlemen, is that Calvin messed us all up when he chose to use the word 'predestination' and then went and carried through with a bunch of stuff on the basis of that word.

"And things would've been simpler and plainer and easier to get hold of if he'd called his basically good idea 'foreknowledge' instead of predestination."

"I'm still confused," Eli said.

"So was I. But let me modify and kinda paraphrase what Calvin was trying to tell us. He got a little off track, I think, when he started listening to himself say predestination. Carried it further than the Word says it goes.

"What I think the Word says is that God *knows* what man is gonna do. Knows it before man is conceived or born. But God also gives us *choice*. Which it says in the Book.

"You see, if we thought of Calvin's ideas as starting from a premise of foreknowledge instead of predestination, I think the whole thing would come clear nice and easy.

"Because there's a difference, a real *big* difference, between God *knowing* what Billy Ray Halstad is gonna do and God *demanding* what Billy Ray Halstad is going to do in his life. The same difference between Him knowing what Ad Smits or Eli Pieck will do and God ordering Ad and Eli to soar in heaven or singe in hell.

"You might call it the doctrine of foreknowledge, if you like. And it works like this . . .

"Imagine there is an innocent child, as we all are in God's sight anyhow, all of us young and dumb compared to Him. Right?"

The deacons nodded.

"Right. So imagine this young, trusting, wide-eyed kid. And imagine him on a Christmas morning when his folks are giving presents out in remembrance of the gifts the magi gave to the infant Jesus.

"And imagine that this child comes down from the loft, and over by the fireplace there are two presents. And this child is allowed to *choose* between them. Which is kinda like the Wesleyan notion of things, where the Calvinist notion would say that the child has no choice but is given one thing and only one, whether that's the thing he wants or not. But for the sake of this example, let's go with Wesley and say that the child is allowed to choose between these two gifts. He has the free will to pick either one of them.

"And the one present he is offered is the hard and thorny path that leads to salvation. The other is the gay, downhill path that leads him to hell. Now put that way, a sensible child would choose salvation. Except we in this life aren't always sensible. And we don't always see things the way they actually are, at least not right off.

"So for the sake of this example, let's imagine this toddler coming down from the loft, and the presents he gets to pick between are two.

"One is a Christmas stocking. Oh, it's a huge thing. Tall as a Clydesdale horse and bulging with goodies. He can see that it holds oranges and lemons and candied apples. If he picks it he'll have tin whistles and toy drums and a bright red shirt to wear around town and show off to the other children, and his eyes get big when he looks at it.

"And the other present, it's a small, drab little envelope of paper, and all it holds is another piece of paper. And the child, he's too young and uninformed to realize that the paper in that envelope is the deed to a grand manor and a huge, sprawling farm that will keep him in comfort for all his days.

"Now, given those two presents to choose from, which is a child gonna take, Ad?"

"The gaudy, shiny baubles, of course."

"Of course he will," Billy Ray said happily. "And it's the same with God and this notion not of predestination but of foreknowledge.

"God *knows* which present that child is gonna take. But the child does have a genuine *choice* in the matter.

"And what God is doing in the background is whispering in that little child's ear . . . which is you and me and each and every one of us on this earth . . . and telling him that it would be better to take the gift that isn't shiny but is true. And *some* of us hear and listen and obey Him. And some of us don't.

"And *that*, gentlemen, is Billy Ray Halstad's doctrine of foreknowledge, and why I say there really isn't such a big conflict between free will and predestination as everybody wants to think. Because each of those has pieces of the truth in it but has gotten all discombobulated with words where it really ought to be simple and straightforward."

Ad Smits frowned and pulled at his jaw. Eli Pieck looked thoughtful.

"I wanta think about this some," Smits said.

"You do that, Ad. You too, Eli. And whatever you think, remember that you don't have to worry about it or think about it all that much, because it doesn't really matter if you or me or any mere man is right. God is right. That's all that really counts."

Billy Ray stood and left the deacons sitting there in the back of the church.

They weren't arguing now. That probably counted for something, he decided.

Next week they would probably explain to him where he was all wet in his ideas. But that was all right too. God was still right, whether Billy Ray Halstad was or not.

37

Billy Ray mumbled something. It was probably a good thing no one was close enough to hear. What he said wasn't the sort of thing a preacher should be saying.

He frowned and watched the Elwick wagon roll out of town with Emmy's curly, blonde-capped head in the back. Her father seemed in even more than his usual hurry today.

Billy Ray sighed. A fellow wouldn't ordinarily think there would be so much trouble involved in so small a matter as just trying to find ten seconds to talk with a member of the congregation. Every time Billy Ray thought he was going to get a moment with Emmy, her father dragged her off again. Not deliberately though, of course. Will and Ethel couldn't know that he wanted to talk with their daughter. The whole thing was supposed to be hush-hush and private. Whatever it was about. Something childish, probably. But something of sincere concern to the child for all of that. Billy Ray shrugged and continued on to Walker Ayers's store.

He didn't really *need* anything there. He just didn't feel like going home to the empty, silent dugout quite yet. Billy Ray had never spent so much time with only himself for company as since he came here to Purgatory City. Not in his whole life.

Mr. Ayers and the other merchants were doing a brisk, if brief, trade with the Sunday-after-church farm crowd.

Billy Ray still found it odd how the farmers shopped on one day and the ranchers on another. And especially odd that the people from his congregation had a get-and-git approach to their shopping. They moved into the stores and right back out again. No time for visiting. No socializing. No talking. It was all a matter of sit and listen to whatever he wanted to tell them, then hurry into town to grab and go again.

He didn't feel particularly close to these people yet. Heck, he didn't feel yet that he really knew them.

He really needed to visit with them, he decided.

Billy Ray's expression and resolve firmed. This week, he decided.

The work on the roof could wait a day or two. No one seemed to appreciate — appreciate? they hadn't seemed to *notice* — the work he had done on the church building so far anyway. It wouldn't matter if the roofing was delayed a little.

This week, by golly, he would go do some visiting in the homes.

He didn't have a horse or rig? Fine. He would walk out and see them. It couldn't be so very far away if they were driving to town in time to be there early Sunday mornings. He would just jolly well walk out and visit with whichever families of them he could reach in a day's time.

Hopefully he would find the Elwick farm and be able to talk to Emmy then too.

He smiled, pleased with the idea.

"Afternoon, Mr. Ayres," he said as he entered the store.

For some reason Mr. Ayres chuckled when he looked up and saw who the visitor was.

"Something funny?" Billy Ray asked.

"Nope," Ayres said quickly. But there was amusement in his eyes when he said it.

Billy Ray shrugged and wandered over to the pickle barrel. He was tempted. A tart, sour pickle was just the ticket when a fellow was eating a bland diet of boiled rice and

193

boiled potatoes and field corn boiled until the kernels were soft enough that they would break before a tooth did. It was a good thing Billy Ray had figured out how to boil water or he'd be in a heck of a mess. He hadn't yet attempted frying anything. Maybe he should give it a shot sometime.

"How much for a pickle?" he asked. He had his eye on a real monster of a sour pickle that was floating fat and heavy just under the surface of the brine.

"No charge," Mr. Ayres said.

"I couldn't do that."

"My treat. Really."

"Thanks." Instead of hauling out the monster, though, he took the tongs and picked out one that he thought would probably be rejected by the paying customers anyway.

"Man, that's good." He grinned and wiped a trickle of juice off his chin.

"Have another."

"Thanks, but one is fine."

"Whatever you say, preacher."

"Billy Ray," Billy Ray corrected.

"Fair enough, Billy Ray," Mr. Ayres said. "Call me Walker."

"Why, thanks."

Walker Ayres chuckled again, for some reason.

Billy Ray finished his pickle and admired the stock on the shelves, none of which had changed in the slightest since the first time he walked inside the place, and then went back out into the sunshine with a wave and a good-bye.

He still wondered what Mr. Ayres found so dang amusing.

He yawned and started ambling back toward the dugout, wondering if there was any chance that Denise might be down by the river this evening.

The truth was that he was having mixed feelings about that. He wanted to see her again. But he wanted to see her again more than he really ought.

After all, she was having feelings for some da . . . ng cowboy. And he was having night thoughts that weren't at all what they should be.

He heard a clatter of horse hooves behind him, so he veered toward the side of the street where he wouldn't be in the way.

The sounds of the horses veered with him and stopped right behind him.

"Yes?" He grinned. "Oh. It's you."

There were three riders in the bunch. Two of them were the cowboys he'd had the little set-to with yesterday. The other was a much older man, well dressed and dignified, who he guessed would be either their dad or their boss.

He was sure neither of those ol' boys on horseback was going to want to step down and jump him. They should've already had enough of that idea.

And the older man looked like he should have enough in the way of age and wisdom to have gone beyond street brawling as a sport.

"Something I can do for you fellas?"

The two cowboys didn't meet his eyes. They were busy fidgeting with their horses' reins or whatever. It was the older man who was giving Billy Ray a stare.

Well, Billy Ray could stare right along with the best of them. He stood where he was and let the fellow have all the looking he wanted.

"You're a funny damn kind of preacher," the older man said after a bit.

"Hilarious," Billy Ray agreed.

"I thought you preachers were all supposed to be limp-wristed little squirts."

"Yeah, I've heard that too. Ain't it a shame how you can't believe everything you hear anymore." Billy Ray grinned up at the cowman. "But I did turn the other cheek for them. They tell you that part of it?"

"They told me."

"Good. Those boys might be dumb, believing like you did that preachers have to be meek, but at least they're no liars. I take it they work for you?"

The cowman nodded.

"You want to tell me what your complaint is?"

"I don't like farmers," he said.

"Shucks. I don't like beets, mister. That doesn't mean I think they oughta be kept out of this whole town. Just off my table."

"I don't like you either," the cowman declared.

Billy Ray grinned. "That's okay. Jesus loves you. If He thinks that much of you, mister, I expect I can take His word about you."

The cowman turned red.

"See?" one of the cowboys complained. "What the hell'd I tell you. This guy ain't natural."

"I could get down from here and thrash you, preacher."

"You could all three of you try," Billy Ray said happily. Shee-oot. He'd been wanting some entertainment this afternoon. This gentleman was providing it handsomely.

"Come on, Vern. Remember what the doctor told you about getting yourself worked up. This farmer preacher ain't worth it."

197

Vern growled and grumbled, but he turned his horse away. The two cowboys followed.

Billy Ray chuckled and wandered on home.

He was feeling better today than he had felt in . . . since he came here, he decided.

Now if only Denise happened to show up on the riverbank this evening . . .

38

He saw the little bay mare before he saw
Denise. His heart leaped, and he scowled
down the surge of excitement. No sense in
beating himself in the head. He rearranged
his features into something suitably neutral,
and stepped out of the brush. Denise was
seated on the log in her usual place.

"Hi."

She jumped.

"Deep in thought, huh?"

"Just . . . daydreaming."

"About something nice, I hope."

She smiled. "As a matter of fact, Just Billy
Ray, it was about something nice. Not very
realistic. But nice."

"Good." He smiled and sat on the log
next to her. Not too close, though. He
crossed his legs and laced his hands over his
knee so he could keep them still, and not be
fidgety.

"Do you ever daydream?"

"All the time," he admitted. He refrained

from adding anything about what — or more accurately who — he daydreamed about.

"Papa says daydreaming is stupid. He says it's a waste of time."

"Is your papa right about everything?" She smiled.

Her gaze drifted off over the moving water of the Purgatory, and she sobered. "Have you thought anything more about . . . what I asked you the other day?"

He nodded, realized she wasn't looking at him and said, "Some." Thought about very little else, really.

"And?" She still wasn't looking at him.

"I think . . . mmm, how should I put this. I know you are no hussy, Miss Trumaine. And I think any gentleman would consider himself fortunate to have your favor."

Her head snapped around toward him, and he blushed. This time he was the one who looked away. Dang, this was embarrassing.

"I think you should come right out and tell him," he blurted.

"I couldn't," she said.

"I think you should."

"What if I embarrassed him? What if it offended him? What if he laughed at me? No, never mind that. He wouldn't laugh. He's too nice a gentleman to laugh. But what if . . . I don't know. Just, what if?"

Too nice a gentleman indeed. Drat it. What could he expect, though. Denise wasn't the kind of girl to fall for some drunk or range bum. Of course it would be a nice man. Had to be, if Denise liked him.

"What if he does have the same feelings?" Billy Ray stubbornly, unwillingly persisted. The persistence was purely a matter of duty, though. His heart wasn't in this conversation.

"What if he doesn't?" she countered.

Then he's an idiot. That was what he wanted to say. But he didn't. "What if he does and neither one of you wants to speak up? What if you both have these feelings but you never find out that you do."

She sighed. "What and if are a pair of really horrid words, aren't they?"

Billy Ray smiled. "Yeah. Aren't they."

"You really think I should tell him?"

No, he wanted to shout.

"I swear I think I would die of embarrassment before I could come right out and say anything."

How odd that a girl as pretty as Denise would be shy. You tended to think of pretty people as being confident and sure of themselves. Denise was the prettiest girl Billy

Ray had ever seen, yet she was as shy as a churchmouse. Which, come to think of it, was a most inappropriate simile under these particular circumstances.

"So don't come right out and say it. I mean, don't fling yourself onto his chest or anything. But you could kind of sneak around the subject. Hint, sort of."

She sighed again. "Sometimes it's awfully hard to know what to do."

"Yeah. Isn't *that* the truth."

"I don't . . . I think I better go home now. I'll think about what you said."

Leave it be, he wanted to shout. Just . . . keep coming here, meeting on the river-bank, sitting and talking over the sounds of the water. Just keep coming and sitting under the leaves in the shade of the cotton-woods.

Except that wasn't any answer either. Not for anybody.

Daydream? That was one. And a stupid one, at that. Every bit as stupid as Denise's father said daydreams were supposed to be. Heck, maybe her father was right about that after all.

"Sure. Think about it. But don't do anything that you're uncomfortable with. Think it through and then do what will make you happy."

"Thank you, Just Billy Ray."

He was looking out across the river. He felt the movement as she stood. She remained there for several long moments. Standing. Not moving. But not speaking.

After a bit she turned and slipped away. He heard the creak of leather as she mounted, and the sound of the little mare moving through the brush.

Billy Ray continued to stare off into the dusk toward the south of the slow-moving river.

"You do ask a lot from Your servants, don't You, Boss."

39

Bright and early Monday morning, Billy Ray stood and surveyed his piles of materials.

He had approximately a mountain's worth of flattened tin cans, every one he could find in the town dump, and a good gallon and a half of nails, brads, staples and tacks. He had scraps of crate sides and lathing to fill in the gaps of thin air that existed between all too many of the old supports.

But all of that would still be there tomorrow, or whenever else he started work on the church roof.

People were more important than things, he told himself righteously.

And he needed to become acquainted with the people of the congregation much more than he needed to repair the church roof.

Putting that off would not really accomplish anything.

Besides, he admitted ruefully, if he was

going to have to put one task off anyway, it might as well be the roofing. He did truly hate and despise and fear the idea of climbing around up there so far off the ground.

So today would probably be a very good day to start his program of visiting.

That settled, he smiled and went back to the dugout for his coat and a breakfast of boiled rice. A preacher should be properly dressed for visiting. And inwardly fortified as well.

He ate quickly. He wasn't particularly hungry after a restless, sleepless night that had left him with burning eyes and an aching head and no end in sight to any of the discomfort.

Probably the decent and sensible and honorable thing to do here would be to submit a resignation from the pulpit. Before Deacon Pieck and Deacon Smits and the rest of the congregation wised up and demanded one.

Except, dang it, if the Boss had sent him here for some purpose, this was where he was supposed to be.

Not that *he* could figure it out.

"I'm really not trying to complain," he said aloud. "But I sure am confused by what You got in mind here."

He picked up his Bible and headed out the door.

Billy Ray had little notion of where his congregation's farms lay except that they were somewhere to the east from town.

There was a road of sorts lying along the river course. If he just followed that he ought to find one place or another. From any one of them he ought to be able to get directions to the next.

He set out walking, the morning sun bright in his eyes, so that he snugged the brim of his cap lower.

Maybe this visiting wasn't such a good idea after all.

The sun wasn't in his eyes any longer. Not hardly. Now it was high overhead. And still he was walking east with no sign yet of any farms.

He passed cattle and cow trails. Antelope. Rabbits. The occasional deer or coyote.

But no plowed fields and no farmhouses and certainly no people.

How far away did these folks live?

He'd been walking a good four hours and still the ruts of the wagon road stretched out in front of him in loops and curves that followed the Purgatory.

His initial jaunty pace had slowed now to

a slow trudge that raised dust off the road surface as his shoe soles scraped across the dry earth.

His feet hurt, his shoes pinched and he was commencing to get hungry too.

He carried his coat in one hand and his Bible in the other, and each felt like it had quadrupled in weight since he left the dugout this morning.

When he judged it was noon, he left the road and went over to the river. The banks were shallow here and barren. There was no longer any of the familiar brush sprouting out of the gravel, and the last of the tall, shading cottonwoods had been left behind more than an hour ago.

Billy Ray didn't know much about land, but this particular piece of it didn't look like much.

It was nearly bare, the sun-cracked earth showing through between isolated clumps of brown, drying grasses.

Ground like this looked to his inexpert eye like it might support an impoverished colony of mice. But not much more than that.

To north and south alike there were harsh and rugged bluffs — or would they be called buttes here, or possibly mesas, he wasn't sure — that were red and gray. And dry.

Except for the presence of the Purgatory,

he doubted that much of anything could survive here.

Even with the river there was little enough that lived. The further he went, the less life he saw around him.

There weren't even very many birds in the air here, and those few that he did see were mostly predators or carrion eaters.

He had thought Purgatory City was in desolate country. But that was before he saw this.

He took a short break, drank deeply from the river and rested his feet for a moment.

Then he picked up his Bible and shouldered his coat and marched on toward the east.

There was something to be said about the idea of crawling around atop a rickety roof after all, he decided.

40

It was afternoon for some time before Billy Ray followed yet another looping curve in the Purgatory, and came out onto an ancient floodplain where the land was a little flatter and the soil a little darker. And where, best of all, there was a farm.

He felt like shouting Hallelujah. Thought about it. And dang sure did. Right out loud.

His voice startled a magpie out of the riverbed, but no one and nothing else seemed to care.

It was no wonder the folks of the congregation got their shopping done and headed home quick as they could on Sabbath afternoons, he decided. Leaving when they did, they would barely have time enough to get home and do their choring before dark.

As for being there early enough to start the services, well, they must be leaving their homes in the pitch dark of the predawn to get there on time, and driving for hours just so they could sit through one of his rotten sermons.

He'd begun to think that the people of this congregation were lukewarm toward the Lord because they didn't hang around to socialize. Huh! Mistakes like that were what a fella got for thinking. Especially when he didn't have all the facts to hand.

Billy Ray tipped his head back and his eyes up and said, "Keep me straight, Lord. You know I got a lot to learn yet."

He hiked the last half mile or so in considerably better spirits than he'd felt in some hours now. Why, even his feet didn't hurt so bad anymore.

Billy Ray was grinning when he got to the farmhouse door. He had no idea whose place he had come to, and it really didn't matter. He was happy to be here.

It was young Mrs. Martin. Charity. Her husband's name was Sam. And the toddler peeping out from behind Mrs. Martin's skirts was Anna. Billy Ray was finally starting to get the names of his flock straight, although he was still having trouble with the relationships. He thought Mrs. Martin was related somehow to Ad Smits's wife, but he wasn't entirely sure about that. He smiled and removed his cap. "Ma'am."

"Why . . . Reverend?" She seemed quite flustered.

"Am I disturbing anything, Mrs. Martin? I can come again some other time."

"No. Please. Come in. Let me get Sam." She motioned him inside, grabbed up little Anna and fled off toward the field where Billy Ray had seen a man swinging a scythe and cradle and stacking a grain crop of some sort. Billy Ray didn't know enough about farms and farming to tell what kind of crop it was.

He chuckled and went inside. He stood there awkwardly, not wanting to take a seat uninvited, and waited patiently for Sam to come in from the field. He hoped he wasn't doing anything bad by interrupting the man's work this afternoon.

Nice folks, Billy Ray reflected as he left the Martin farm. They'd seemed genuinely pleased to see him, once they got over the surprise and realized the visit wasn't for any emergency purpose. There'd never been a preacher visit in their home before, they'd said. Or at any of the other places that they knew about. In fact, they never had company of any kind very much. They'd gone out of their way to make him feel welcome.

All in all, a pleasant visit. They'd talked a

little, prayed a little, told him about themselves and their baby and their dreams for
the future. That was what it was all about,
wasn't it. He felt warm and smiley as he
headed toward the next place.

Now that he was this far, he figured he
needed to visit as many families as he could
reach. This wasn't a walk he was going to
want to make all too frequently.

And now that he was this far, he hadn't
much further to go to reach any of the
farms.

They were all clustered fairly close together now, strung out along both sides of
the river. And Sam and Charity Martin had
told him where to find each of the other
families' places.

The Elwick farm, thank goodness, was
this side of the Purgatory.

There was a ford where a man could cross
afoot, they'd said, but Billy Ray didn't want
to get his trouser legs wet and then have to
make the long walk back to town that way.
He would have if he'd had to, but he was
glad it wasn't necessary. Another time,
when he could arrive in the vicinity earlier,
he thought.

He hiked on. Stopped briefly at the Smits
farm. Stopped again at the Grundle place
and Andrews'. He would have enjoyed vis-

iting with Eli Pieck, but Eli lived on the easternmost farm this side of the river, and it was already late in the afternoon by the time Billy Ray reached the Elwick place. This visiting was time-consuming. Once he got in a place, they wanted to load him up with coffee and bread or whatever else they had on hand, and keep him there awhile. If he'd been hungry to begin with, and he had, he'd certainly had that need well taken care of since.

He approached the Elwick farm with a grin and a wave. Ethel was outside taking freshly washed and dried clothes down off the line. By now he was expecting to see both the surprise and the pleasure on her features when he came into view.

"Reverend!"

"Yes, ma'am. I hope I'm not interrupting?"

"Come in. Please. Will has taken our team over to help Mr. Krohn clean out his water ditch. Oh, dear. Should I . . . do you want me to run and get him?"

"Don't bother. I'm just stopping by. I don't have any bad news. Just wanted to visit a little and get acquainted."

"You must come in. I have some tea water handy. And you'll have a cruller? They aren't fresh, though. They've been setting

213

since morning. Oh, dear. I should make some fresh. I should . . ."

He laughed and stopped her. "Please, now. I don't want to be a bother. I just wanted to say hello."

"Emmy? Emmaline! Where are you?"

The child, really Billy Ray's main reason for wanting to make the walk out from town, popped out of a low, sapling-roofed chicken shed with a bulging, egg-heavy kerchief bundled in her hand. "Yes, Mama?" She saw the preacher and grinned. He could see in her eyes that she knew already why he'd come.

Yeah, he thought. That made all the walking worthwhile.

"Come inside, honey. The reverend has come to pay us a call."

Emmy gathered her skirt high with her one free hand and came loping across the bare, dusty farmyard to join them.

41

Billy Ray wanted to sit down something awful. His feet were hurting after so much walking, but here in the chicken coop there was nothing to sit on except the pole roost, and that was layered deep with droppings from the hens.

He had come out to the coop with Emmy on the pretext of helping her gather the last of the eggs. She'd been interrupted in the chore by his arrival earlier.

Ethel was absolutely insisting that he stay to dinner with them. Will would be crushed, she swore, if the preacher was right there in their home and Will didn't get to see him and have prayer with him. He really *had* to stay, she swore. And Will would be home soon. Before dark, and that was soon, wasn't it.

So Billy Ray agreed and suggested that he help Emmy, and now he was standing hunched over under a roof that was high enough to accommodate Emmy's stature but certainly not a grown man's.

"You're an awfully hard person to have a word with in private," he told the little girl gently.

"You haven't said anything? Not to anybody?"

"Not a word. Not to a soul," he assured her. "What's more, Emmy, I won't say anything."

"Not even to Papa?"

"Not even. I'll talk to you about whatever you want. And I'll tell you what I think. If it's something that needs praying about, I'll pray on it. But whatever it is, the Lord knows about it already. That won't be breaking any secrets."

"I know." She looked unhappy now. "Jesus already does know, don't He?"

"He sure does, Emmy. But I can promise you I won't say anything to anybody except Jesus. Not unless you say I can."

"Promise?"

"Promise."

She took a deep breath. "I sinned, Reverend. I done a terrible sin, and I'm sorry for it, and Deacon Smits says if anybody sins they're gonna burn in hell forever and always. And I don't want to go to hell, Reverend." Her face twisted, and she began to cry. "I truly don't, and I'm sorry, and I don't want to go to hell, but it's too late now t' call back what I did, and . . ."

Billy Ray put an arm around her and drew the sobbing child tight against his chest. He petted and stroked her and told her over and over to settle down, calm down, take it easy now.

When the tears and the sobbing slowed, he bent lower so he could look the little girl in the eyes.

"First off, Emmy, and mind that I don't know yet what your sin was, first off, the Lord is willing to *forgive* sins. That's what salvation is all about, Emmy. Have you forgotten that?"

"I haven't forgot, Reverend. But this wasn't some regular kinda sin. It wasn't like forgetting to make my bed or letting the corn cakes burn or not refilling the kindling box. This was a real *serious* sin."

"As serious as . . . stealing? Was it that serious a sin, Emmy?" Swiping was something a youngster might do, he thought.

"No, sir. I expect it wasn't *that* serious."

He felt easier, knowing Emmy's sin wasn't really a very serious problem, however dark and serious she seemed to find it. "Do you remember hearing about when Jesus was crucified, Emmy? When He was hung on the cross to die for all our sins?"

"Of course," she said indignantly.

"Remember I asked if what you did was as serious as stealing? Well, when Jesus was crucified that day at Calvary, Emmy, He wasn't the only one on a cross. You remember that, don't you?"

"Yes. I think so."

"Well, He wasn't, Emmy. There were two men crucified with Him, one on each side of Him, just like the prophesy said there would be. And those two men were thieves. They were such bad thieves that they were being put to death for their crimes. Kind of like somebody being hanged nowadays. And do you remember that just because he believed in Jesus and put his faith in Jesus and repented, one of those thieves that day was saved from all his sins and promised a place in heaven. Jesus personally made that promise to a thief. But the other thief, who didn't believe in Jesus, he died and I expect he did go to hell, Emmy. The Lord forgives every kind of sin, Emmy. Thieving. Murder. Even worse than that. If we just trust Him to do it. So let me ask you this. Do you believe in Jesus?"

"Of course."

"Are you sorry you sinned?"

"Yes."

"Well, that takes care of that, Emmy.

Jesus will forgive you for your sins. That's all it takes." He smiled.

Emmy's eyes dropped away from his.

"What if I do it again, Reverend?" she whispered. "What if I do this same sin again?"

"Mm. I think maybe we need to talk about this some more."

"I know," she said seriously.

Billy Ray couldn't laugh until he was well away from the Elwick home, his stomach full and his spirits uplifted.

Lordy, the things kids could come up with and think they were hell-bound because of it.

Once he was out of sight on the long road back to town and with the night wrapped tight around him, he let it out and laughed aloud.

"Thanks for helping me, Boss," he added. And chuckled again.

Such a *serious* sin little Emmy had committed.

She'd let Aaron Andrews, who couldn't be more than six months older than Emmy, *kiss* her. Right *there*. On the side of her lips. Practically on the mouth. And that was a sin. Everybody knew that. But she'd *liked* it. Emmy wanted Aaron to kiss her *again*.

Billy Ray grinned. Emmy admitted right out that she wanted Aaron to kiss her again *almost* as much as she wanted to avoid going to hell.

He laughed. So serious a sin, so serious a problem. Although of course at that age the problem was a real and perplexing one.

Little Emmy had been fretting and stewing about this for weeks, bless her heart. Literally for weeks. Since before she thought to try and ask the new preacher about it.

And poor Aaron. According to Emmy, he was wanting to kiss her again but she wouldn't let him.

Billy Ray wished all his problems were so easy to solve.

"God understands about boys and girls liking each other, Emmy," he'd explained to her. "Why, it's God who made us and put these feelings inside us. It's His proper plan that we feel the way we do. Those feelings are what leads us to marriage and children and love of family, and all those things go right along hand in hand with our love for God. A kiss on the lips, Emmy, that won't send anybody to hell. It's when we misuse our bodies and are wicked and wanton that we've sinned against God. And if we do do wrong and sin, He's still willing to forgive us an honest repentance. But a kiss by itself, that isn't a sin. And neither is the things we feel toward another person. Because all of that is part of God's plan for us."

"You're sure?"

"Absolutely." He hoped, though, that she didn't want to see it in black and white, because right off-hand he couldn't think of where to look to prove the point to her. He could look up kissing in the concordance, he supposed. But he couldn't honestly claim that that was the sort of kissing Emmy had in mind when young Aaron Andrews was in her thoughts.

Sometimes you just had to try and work things out the long way around, instead of getting it all cut and neatly dried for you.

It was chilly now that the sun was down, even with the heat of the exercise.

Billy Ray paused for a moment to pull his coat on, glad now that he'd brought it, and stepped out at a brisk pace when he resumed his trek back toward town.

42

He was tired. His feet hurt. And he had long since gone past chilly. Now he was positively freezing.

It was hard to believe that a day that had been so sunny and nice had gone and turned now into a night so bitterly cold.

It didn't help a thing that a strong, steady wind had come up, blowing out of the north and driving through the material of Billy Ray's coat and trousers and thin, fraying, second-best shirt.

This was *not* one of the most fun things he'd done lately.

He turned and looked back along the curving bed of the Purgatory.

The last lights of the farm settlement had disappeared behind him more than an hour ago. Even so, he was half tempted to go back.

The Elwicks had offered him a pallet to sleep on. So for that matter had everyone else. It was only pride and a hint of shyness that made him insist on going home tonight. He had work to do on the church, after all. And he wouldn't have been comfortable sleeping in strange surroundings with other people there so close by. What if he snored? That sort of thing never used to occur to him back when he bunked in a mining-town boarding house in long, barracklike rooms filled with other working stiffs. For several years now, though, he had become used to the idea of privacy. He liked it. Too well, perhaps.

Billy Ray sighed and trudged on into the night with his coat collar turned as high as it would go and his cap pulled low to his ears, his one free hand stuffed into a pocket.

He would have been more comfortable if his Bible had been small enough to slip into a pocket. Then he could have protected both hands at once. This way one hand was always exposed and entirely too cold. His knuckles ached, and his fingertips tingled. He wondered just how cold it was going to get tonight.

"You wouldn't care to send me a passing carriage, would You?" he asked.

After a moment he added, "I didn't think so."

It was one thing when a guy's feet hurt. It

was another when his calves ached and his knees felt rubbery. How the heck many miles had he walked today, anyway. He didn't want to guess.

He sat on a shelf of pale, gritty rock and shivered.

The road and the river lay in a long, sweeping curve before him, the path dimly visible in the pale moonlight.

If he remembered correctly, the river here took a deep bend to the south, and the farmers' wagon road paralleled it.

He could save himself, he bet, two, three miles of walking if he cut straight across the inside of the curve. Like putting a string on a bow.

Right now he would consider it a blessing from the Lord if he could save a hundred yards of walking, much less several miles of it.

All he would have to do here would be to walk straight west from this point. He would meet up with the river and the road right over there a little ways.

And by that point there should be a line of brush and trees marking the riverbed again, so it would be easy to spot even in the moonlight.

The stars off to the west would point his way.

There was no chance of getting lost.

Billy Ray grunted softly to himself and stood, his feet and lower legs paining him after the brief halt. He actually hated having to put his weight back onto his feet again.

No choice about that now, of course.

"Just a little further. Right, Lord?"

He angled off the south-curving road and headed straight west.

43

The second time he fell down, Billy Ray began to get worried. If he twisted an ankle or, worse, actually broke something in a fall . . .

The wind had driven a thick cover of cloud down from the north, obscuring the moon that was supposed to light his way and the stars that were supposed to guide it.

The country was rocky here and ran more to up-and-down than to the level flats he'd been expecting.

He couldn't see where he was walking. Didn't have legs steady enough to feel his way along. And he was starting to get scared.

That was the simple truth of the matter. He was getting scared.

He could hear coyotes yelping in front of him, and another pack of them answering from somewhere to the left.

Coyotes weren't supposed to bother people. That's what everybody said.

What the heck did *everybody* know?

Somebody saying the creatures were harmless didn't make them that way.

They always looked to Billy Ray like undersized wolves. And everybody — different everybody this time — knew what wolves were like.

Heck, up in the mountains Billy Ray had even heard fellows say in all seriousness how the black bears were harmless; it was only the grizzlies you had to watch out for.

Shee-oot. Who was going to ask a bear its ancestry if you came up face to face with one.

Same thing with coyotes, as far as he was concerned. He didn't like them; he didn't trust them, and he darn sure didn't want to be the one person in the whole of recorded history who would end up disproving this theory about the flea-bitten little beasts being harmless.

They *sounded* harmful. Billy Ray Halstad had no intention of investigating any deeper than that.

He gathered himself into a sitting position, since he happened to be on the ground anyway, and didn't even worry at the moment about what he might have done to the knees of his pants when he fell.

It felt so good to get off his feet for a

moment that it was almost a relief to have fallen.

He groaned and sank down against the earth.

What he wanted, really, was a bed of soft loam and sweet-smelling grass that he could lie back against. And oh yes, some warmth to enjoy it in.

Instead he was being poked by rocks and annoyed by gravel, and there was a low, spiky cactus right beside him that he very nearly put a hand down onto.

And he was freezing.

Lordy, but it was bitter cold.

He hoped there wasn't any snow inside those clouds overhead. He had no idea what time of year a body could expect snow around here. In the mountains that could be anytime at all except *maybe* the last week of July and the first week of August. But there weren't any guarantees even about that. Down here in the flatland he just didn't know.

"You got a good reason for doing this?" he asked aloud. "I mean, I don't mean to complain, Boss. But I'd sure take to it easier if You got something particular in mind."

His only answer was a gust of wind that curled inside the collar of his coat and sent a fresh chill shivering through his thin frame.

"Thanks a lot," he said.

There wasn't any point in trying to keep the bitterness out of his voice. The Lord already knew what Billy Ray was thinking anyhow.

44

Billy Ray woke to a red gleam behind his eyelids. His first thought was that he couldn't believe he had actually fallen asleep. His second was relief that it was finally dawn.

There was a thin sliver of red-orange sun creeping over the eastern horizon.

The sun wasn't warm yet. But at least he could see now if any coyote tried to sneak up on him.

He sat up, shivering, and looked around.

There was nothing but barren, rocky desolation in any direction he could see.

He must have climbed more than he'd realized last night. He was halfway up a loaf-shaped bench of earth and rock.

He could see for miles to east and south and west, and all he could see in any of those directions was more rock and more bare dirt and an occasional sprig of cactus or yucca or sage.

This was desert. It was actual dang desert. Or as close to it as Billy Ray wanted to get.

He shivered again and tried to draw some warmth by wrapping his own arms tight around himself.

Jesus had gone out into the desert, hadn't He?

Spent forty *days* in the wilderness. And forty cold nights.

Billy Ray shuddered.

Forty days.

Billy Ray Halstad was a mess after one lone, miserable night in this desert.

His feet hurt, his legs ached and his belly was rumbling with hunger.

And Jesus had spent forty days doing this?

He picked up his Bible and leafed into it. Luke, he thought. Right. But not so far into the book as he'd thought. Fourth chapter. There it was, right there.

Forty days in the wilderness with nothing to eat, and the devil tempting Him and trying to offer Him bread made out of stones — that was where the "not by bread alone" passage that everybody recalled, but not so many remembered exactly from where, that was where that one came from — and offering Him all manner of worldly power and glory.

Forty days. Wow.

And that was where — he looked it up;

eighth verse — another much remembered phrase came from. When Jesus told Satan to buzz off and go bother somebody else. "Get thee behind me, Satan; for it is written, Thou shalt worship the Lord thy God; and Him only shalt thou serve."

"Ha!" Billy Ray barked aloud.

He stood, Bible in hand, and brushed himself off.

Forty days like this and worse than this.

Why, shoot, to get out of his wilderness all Billy Ray had to do was walk south — he could figure that out now that the sun had come up — until he hit the north bank of the Purgatory, and turn right. He'd be home in no time.

Billy Ray snapped his Bible closed and grinned.

"Get thee behind me, Satan," he bellowed into the bright, rosy light of the new dawn. "Get thee behind me and *stay* there."

45

Billy Ray still felt dragged-out and sore when he woke the next morning — in his own bed, thank goodness — even after half a day of laziness and a full night's sleep.

He gimped on aching legs to the doorway, long enough to ascertain that the sun had successfully come up again and to give the church roof a looking-over from afar. One more day wasn't going to make all that much difference, he decided.

He went back inside the dugout for a huge breakfast of cornmeal mush — cornmeal boiled with a little salt and lard added to the pot, which didn't taste a whole lot like the mush he remembered having as a boy, but which was as close as he knew how to come to it — and then spent the rest of the morning in laziness again, Bible open on his lap and his feet propped up. It was amazing how poorly a person could get to feeling after one single night in a wilderness.

By noon he felt up to walking over to town

for one of Mr. Ayres's pickles. If he didn't watch himself, he thought, he just might become addicted to those crisp, tart, sour pickles.

He cur across the back of the main-street buildings and emerged onto the street as a group of riders were leaving the store.

Billy Ray stopped and drew back into the alley he had just passed through.

Denise was with them. Riding the familiar little bay mare she favored.

She hadn't been down to the riverbank last night. Billy Ray had waited on the log there, hoping she would come along, for nearly two hours.

Now . . . She was riding next to the cowman who had wanted to brace Billy Ray on Sunday. Vern, the cowboys had called him.

Oh, Lordy. Not him!

Billy Ray felt cold.

An older man, she'd said.

A gentleman, she'd said.

Oh, Lord.

That was the man Denise Trumaine wanted to give her heart to.

Vern was the man she was coming to Billy Ray for advice about.

And he had gone and told her she should own up to her feelings.

Nice, she'd said of Vern. Billy Ray grimaced. Right. You bet. A nice man who hated farmers and wanted his hired hands to beat up on a weak, wimpy preacher because having the church here encouraged the farmers. Yeah, that was plenty nice, wasn't it.

Well, he couldn't say anything to her about it now. That would be no more than sour grapes.

The advice he'd given her when she asked had been honest, if nothing else.

No matter that he was regretting it now. He'd answered the girl as honestly as he'd known how.

He couldn't take that back because of his own stupid feelings.

But he didn't have to like it either.

He watched from the alley across the street as Denise laughed at something Vern said.

She laughed that sweet, bell-like laugh Billy Ray liked so very much to hear, and Vern helped her onto the mare and mounted his own horse beside her.

He said something more, and Denise laughed again. She reached over and squeezed the wrist of Vern's rein hand.

Billy Ray's heart turned to lead and dropped into his belly.

Denise must have taken his advice, then.

She'd talked to Vern about her feelings.

And like any sensible human male person, Vern knew beauty and quality when he saw it.

Naturally he reciprocated Denise's feelings.

Anybody lucky enough to find favor in Denise Trumaine's eyes would surely have to return her feelings. It wouldn't be natural for it to be otherwise.

Denise giggled and said something, and Vern laughed.

The two of them and the pair of cowboys riding with them headed their mounts down the street toward the west. Away from Purgatory City and away from a hurting, blindly yearning Billy Ray.

Billy Ray turned back toward the dugout. He was no longer interested in one of Mr. Ayres's pickles.

Right now he no longer felt interested in very much of anything.

"Ease up, Lord. Will You? Please?"

He spent the remainder of the day moping, while he pretended to read.

He didn't know who he was supposed to be fooling about that. He knew better and so did the Lord. He just felt too miserable and low to concentrate on anything else.

46

Work on the church roof was progressing.
Slowly.

He didn't have a ladder, and all the discarded crates that he might have piled up to make a platform had already been burned so he could get his supply of nails. He made do with some laboriously chopped saplings and some scrap wood crosspieces that were nailed and wired into place as firmly as he could make them.

The ladder was not something to inspire confidence. But it worked.

It helped considerably that shingling has to be started on the lowest section of the roof and proceeds upward from there.

The fall would be shorter if his makeshift ladder broke early in the game. Or if Billy Ray's nerve broke before the ladder did, and he just screamed his way down to the ground.

Lordy, but he did fear heights. Always had.

If God had intended for man to reach the heights, He'd've given man longer legs, Billy Ray figured.

He nibbled away at the roofing one shaky, sweaty layer at a time, though, and by Saturday evening had about a quarter of one side done.

He'd started on the side of the roof that faced east, so the congregation would see the new steel shingles shining in the sun first thing when they drove in on Sunday morning.

He hoped the Lord would understand that little conceit and not be mad about it.

Saturday night he left the lamp unlighted and stretched out on his cot to do some thinking. He didn't go to the riverbank. He hadn't been there since Wednesday, when he'd seen Denise and Vern together in town. He hadn't been to the river or to town either one since then.

It occurred to him in the night silence that the faults with this church weren't with the flock. They were with the shepherd, dang it.

Billy Ray Halstad wasn't pulling his weight.

He'd been sluggish and self-centered and looking mostly back instead of forward.

The Lord's stony path was forward.

Jesus had spent forty days and forty nights

in a wilderness, hungry and thirsty and with Satan right there at His side tempting and entreating and promising Him all the world, if only Jesus would take the easy path to perdition.

Billy Ray Halstad couldn't hardly cut one single night without a roof overhead.

What he really needed to do, Billy Ray decided, was to get back to the roots of what was right.

Speak not from the Book but from his heart.

Quit trying to sermonize and just *tell* those folks what the truth was.

That was all they needed.

That was all little Emmy Elwick had wanted.

That was what preaching was.

The words would come if a guy had the simple sense to open his heart to the Lord and let the Lord have His way.

Billy Ray smiled and let himself drift off into sleep without the first lick of preparation for tomorrow's sermon.

47

"Hey!"

His voice boomed through the small church building. The congregation hadn't even had time yet to get fully seated and settled.

Heads snapped around. People froze in place. Mrs. Andrews leaped like she had just been stuck with a particularly long and sharp-tipped hatpin.

Billy Ray grinned at them.

"Enough of this long-faced and serious stuff. Who in this church today loves the Lord?"

The folks of Purgatory City looked at him like he'd gone mad.

Well, maybe he had at that. He continued to grin into their stares of blank astonishment. "Who came here today to shout some praise? Don't just sit there! Let me see some hands."

He began to see some smiles now amid the confusion.

"Eli," Billy Ray shouted. "Brother Eli Pieck. Do you love the Lord, Eli?"

The deacon was definitely caught off guard. He blushed as everyone's eyes turned onto him. Then he stammered, "You know I do, Reverend."

"Did you come here today to praise Him, Eli?"

"Well. Yes. I expect you could say that I did, Reverend."

"Put your hand up, Eli. Keep it there." Deacon Pieck did as he was told. Not that he raised his hand particularly high, but he did put it up.

"Ad Smits? Will Elwick? Max . . ." Billy Ray went around the room that way, leaving out no one whose name he could remember and pointing to those, mostly children, whose names would not come immediately to mind.

He didn't quit until everyone in the building was standing now with their hands upraised.

"Good!" Billy Ray declared. "Because that's why I'm here today too." He grinned again. "And while I think about it, my name is Billy Ray. It isn't Reverend; it isn't Pastor; it isn't Preacher. It's just Billy Ray Halstad, and I'm not a lick better than anybody else here this morning. The difference is that

I'm getting paid for doing what every one of you does every day of the week, and that's loving the Lord and praising His name and trying my level best to do what He wants of me. Now put your hands down and sit, and I'll tell you something about myself and why I think the Lord has pointed out the path for you and me and all of us to follow."

Whee-oo.

He was feeling it now. *This* was what had been missing all this time. This soaring, up-lifting, blood-pumping sense of *joy*.

Billy Ray tipped his head back and shouted, "Praise Him!"

He grinned down at the congregation and called, "I don't heee-ear you."

Someone injected a few weak "Amens" and he bobbed his head in encouragement. "That's better. If you love Him, dang it, *tell* Him so."

"Amen," a thin, childish voice from the back called.

"You bet," Billy Ray shouted. "Amen and amen and amen. Do any of you know what 'amen' *means?*"

Nobody said anything.

"It means 'that's right, Boss.' It means 'yeah, I agree with what was said there.' It means 'you bet I think so.' That's what 'amen' means. And from now on, anybody wants to say 'amen,' why, have you at it. Anybody wants to ask a question or make a comment, you speak right up. This here isn't my church. It isn't even your church. It's God's church. And anything any one of His folks want to talk with Him about here, that's what oughta be talked about.

"Now a minute ago I said I'd start off today by telling you about myself. First thing I got to tell you is that I'm a sinner. I'm not going to give you a catalog of all the sins I've done. Because I want to apologize for that, not brag on it. Point is, I'm a sinner. No better than anybody else. *But I've been saved.* The day I got down on my knees and asked the Lord to forgive me, He did just that. He forgave me for my sinning, and He wiped the slate clean so now there isn't a smudge on my page in the Lamb's Book of Life. Have you ever thought about how grand a thing that is? How sweet and pure and good? No? Well, I want you to. And we'll talk about that some more here shortly. But first . . ."

Yeah, this was better.

No notes. No text. No dull, droning boredom of reading. And no fretting or worrying either.

Billy Ray opened his heart to the folks in front of him and let the Spirit flow through.

This was what he was supposed to do with the joy he felt today.

That joy had been missing for what seemed a long time now. Not because the Lord took it away from him, but because Billy Ray Halstad went and stifled it his own self. Worried and fussed it purely out of sight.

He grinned as he spoke until the sides of his jaws ached, and still he kept grinning.

48

The members of the congregation seemed warm and friendly as they left the church this morning. They filed slowly by and pumped Billy Ray's hands and smiled, and once they were past began to cluster near the front of the building instead of hurrying straight to their wagons and the stores and home.

For a change they seemed to want to visit. And not just with Billy Ray but with each other too.

Billy Ray suspected they could feel the joy of the morning as much as he could. Like him, he suspected, they would not want to lose that feeling in exchange for the workaday cares of the week to come.

Virtually everyone complimented him on the service. And virtually everyone added pleased comment as well about the work he had been doing on the church.

The roofing work came in for particular praise.

All this time, he suspected, they had been

pleased but too shy to know if they should say anything to him about it.

Between his visiting with so many of them during the week and now the joyous spirit of the Sunday morning service, they were beginning to relax and open up with him.

They hadn't been standoffish with him, he realized. He had been holding himself apart from them. He was the newcomer here. It was his place to show his worthiness for the trust these folks had placed in him.

He glanced toward the clear, cloud-dotted sky, winked and whispered a brief "Thanks," and went back to shaking hands and grinning and accepting the praise these people tried to heap onto him.

"You're doing a wonderful job on the roof, Reverend," Harold Krohn told him. The tall, gray-haired farmer had Billy Ray's right hand trapped between both of his huge, work-roughed paws, and was pumping it even as he talked.

Billy Ray gave him a look of admonishment.

"Sorry. Billy Ray, I mean."

"That's better, Harold. Thank you."

It occurred to Billy Ray that with everyone so enthused about the progress on the church building, this would be a perfect time to suggest that some of the men come in with ladders and hammers and some roofing nails, if anyone had any lying about in their sheds or barns.

Except that wouldn't be right, he realized. Not really.

These men had farms to work and families to feed and livestock to tend.

They worked dawn to dusk six days out of every week, and spent their Sundays declaring their faith. And driving four or five hours each way to and from town for the privilege of doing so.

It wouldn't be right for Billy Ray Halstad to ask an extra day from them when he had more than enough time to work on the building himself.

If he happened to be afraid of heights and nervous when he was working on the roof, well, it wasn't anything that prayer and faith wouldn't get him through.

Better if he kept his mouth shut on that subject, or tomorrow he would have every farm in the valley left untended.

When the last few folks went outside — the deacons being the last out, as usual — still everyone remained gathered at the front of the church building.

No one seemed quite willing to give up the closeness that had come through them during the service. No one seemed to want to drive away just yet.

"Something I've been thinking," Billy Ray said, and everyone's attention swiveled to him like he was still inside preaching to them. "It's a long drive back for each of you. Surely everyone has to stop and eat somewhere."

Murmured agreement, nods and shrugs met his glance.

"Why don't we all get in the habit of eating here together when the service is over. No obligation, of course. Anyone who has to hurry home or get to the store should go right on. But anybody who has to stop anyway, well, why don't we spend our eating time sharing the Lord's joy too. We can eat indoors when the weather is poor. And I can put up a brush arbor to use when it's fine. It won't cost anything but a little time for me to put some shade over our heads."

"I have some lumber left over from my new coop," Claude Andrews said. "I could make up some trestle tables for under the arbor."

"I'll help you, Claude," Sam Martin said. "An' I can build some benches."

Billy Ray chuckled.

The folks grabbed onto the idea like it had been their own.

Women scattered toward the wagons to

fetch baskets and bundles of foods they had prepared expecting to eat them on the road.

The children whooped and raced about like they'd just gotten a reprieve from confinement, although a temporary and short-lived reprieve, and began inventing games to play.

Billy Ray noticed Emmy Elwick and Aaron Andrews standing in deep conversation near Aaron's parents' wagon.

Emmy and Aaron were only children, but it was not impossible that one of these days in the years that lay ahead Billy Ray might find himself conducting their wedding service. He wished each of them well, whatever the future might bring them.

Billy Ray felt happy for the first time since the Boss had brought him here.

The men lifted the cargo box off Sam Martin's light wagon and upended it to serve as a makeshift cable, and the women covered the grimy, dust-coated lumber with food, laying out everything that had been brought so they could all share of whatever was available in an unplanned potluck dinner.

Billy Ray was so involved in enjoying the sense of community that was developing here that he did not notice the crowd of onlookers that was beginning to grow at the near edge of the town.

Young men wearing large hats and boots with tall, curving heels began to notice and to frown as the churchgoers turned dry sandwiches, intended to be eaten along the road, into a picnic party outside the doors of their no longer dilapidated little church building.

Word about the development seemed to spread until soon there were at least a score of cowboys watching from the distance.

"We're all set to eat, Billy Ray, if you'll say a blessing over this food and the week to come."

"Amen to that," Billy Ray said, as he stepped forward and motioned everyone to silence.

49

"What the hell are you people up to here?"

Billy Ray looked up from the napkin of cold biscuits and hard-boiled eggs Charity Martin had handed him.

There were twenty-five or thirty hard-faced men staring at them, at least a third of the men mounted.

The man who was at the front of the pack — and pack was exactly what Billy Ray thought it was — was the older, richly dressed cowman called Vern. It must have been Vern who had spoken, he guessed.

The grown men and half-grown boys among the farmers stood and began moving their wives and kids off to the far side of the wagon-box table.

Billy Ray stood and motioned the menfolk back to their places.

He grinned up at Vern and said, "This here is something farmers and certain other folks do now and then. It's called dinner. Can you say that? Dinner. Watch my lips. Din-ner."

He probably should have known better than to goad the man like that.

After all, Billy Ray's real problem with this Vern fella was jealousy, pure and simple. This was the guy he'd seen Denise with shortly after he was dumb enough to advise her to express her feelings.

The taunting words came into his head and off his tongue before he had time to think about them.

Worse yet, behind him there was a chorus of laughter from the folks in the congregation who were overhearing.

Vern turned a beety shade of red. Billy Ray got the impression that Vern wasn't much used to being talked to this way.

"Listen you . . ."

"I'd invite you fellas to stay for the pot-luck with us except I don't think we have enough for everybody." Billy Ray looked past Vern toward the cowboys — cowhands — who were with him. "If any of you boys wants to drag some food onto the table you're welcome to eat. Or just set in and visit with us while we finish up. You're always welcome at God's table." He looked at Vern and added, "You too, mister. Sometimes I'm a smart-mouth, but that doesn't mean that the Lord feels the same way about you that I do. Truth is, mister, He loves you as much as He loves me and all these people." He turned and motioned to the farmers. "Shift aside there, folks, and make room for these boys to hunker down beside you."

"That isn't . . ."

"Oh, I know that, Vern. You fellas came over here wanting to cause trouble. That's okay. We'll visit awhile first. There's always time to fight later on."

Vern's mouth gaped like a banked fish sucking air. The cowboys behind him looked back and forth among themselves. They acted uneasy, like they were reluctant to start a tussle now that they'd been invited to dinner.

Billy Ray grinned.

"I don't like you, Halstad. And I don't like farmers," Vern said.

"I thought we'd gone over this once already."

"Those people have taken up my best grass," Vern accused.

Billy Ray laughed. "Mister, I've seen that country they're trying to farm. If that ground out there is the best grass you've got, then I feel almighty sorry for your cows."

"That land was open to the Homestead Act an' you well know it, Mister Tr . . ."

Billy Ray cut the indignant voice off before Ad went and got the fight going again.

"You want me to make you a promise?" Billy Ray asked. "I'll make you one. Any of my flock has been stealing from you, mister, I'll see they give it all back to you. The Boss, He frowns on stealing even worse than you do. But any of this flock that has the lawful right to be where they are and doing what they're doing, that is another matter entirely. Now are you fellas going to join us or not?"

"Go to hell."

"Not me. That's a promise God made to us. He'd make it to you too, if you want."

"Dammit, Vern, do we bust up this bunch or what?" one of the cowboys complained. He was afoot and looked about two-thirds hung over.

"Well, at least have the courtesy to wait until we finish eating," Billy Ray said before Vern could answer.

"You're a smart-alec son of a bitch, aren't you," Vern said. "I have half a mind to turn my boys loose right now."

Billy Ray was still grinning. He set his napkin of food down and took off his coat. "You know, boys, when I got up this morning I sure didn't know how much fun I was fixing to have. What say I start with you, Vern? Or d'you just talk about it and pay others to do everything for you? Are you man enough to have at the preacher, Vern, or do you want to hire a crowd to take care of it for you?"

With everybody, farmers and cowboys alike, looking on, Billy Ray had Vern in a box, and he knew it.

There was a light thunder of horse hooves coming from the direction of town. Reinforcements. Wonderful. The cowboys already outnumbered the male farmers by a good three to one.

"Well?" Billy Ray demanded.

Vern turned even redder than he'd been before, and stepped down from his saddle. The rancher tossed his rein ends to the hung-over cowboy and began pulling his own coat off.

50

Someone shouted in outraged pain, and the rest of the cowboys leaped for safety as a horse came bolting through the pack of men and animals and slid to a halt beside Vern. Derek Trumaine had arrived too, but he yanked his horse to a stop at the back of the crowd.

Billy Ray's heart sank as he saw who the lead rider was.

Denise came flying out of her saddle with a thoroughly immodest show of ankle, and even calf, as her riding skirt swirled.

She looked angry enough to spit.

Billy Ray felt sick.

He had gone and thrown a gauntlet down, dang it. Now he was going to have to eat the thing.

There wasn't any way a fellow Vern's age could stand up to him.

But there wasn't any way either that Billy Ray was going to make Denise watch while the preacher man beat up on her true love.

Billy Ray glanced skyward. "And here I thought You had everything going so nicely today," he muttered.

"Don't you dare," Denise snapped.

Her eyes were flashing and her hair was coming askew from its pins, after the rush of speed on the little bay mare.

"Don't either one of you dare move," she ordered.

"Yes'm," Billy Ray said contritely.

"Denise. Honey!" Vern groaned.

"Don't either one of you dare move an inch."

Billy Ray and Vern were squared off a few paces apart, with Denise right smack in between them.

The girl acted like she didn't know which of them she wanted to glare at first. Her head kept swiveling back and forth between them. She looked like if she puffed up the least little bit fuller with indignation her corset strings were going to snap.

"Honey —"

"Denise —"

"You're both acting like a pair of children," she accused. "Little boys all set to roll and tumble in the schoolyard."

"But, honey . . ."

"Denise —"

"Oh, hush." She turned and pointed a

finger under Billy Ray's nose. "You hush too. Don't you be starting up now. And don't either one of you dare try and tell me who started it."

She looked so mad — and so serious about being mad — that it was almost funny. Billy Ray dang near laughed.

He couldn't help it. He chuckled and pointed a finger and said, "He started it."

Vern didn't see any humor in the situation. He got red in the face all over again. He started for Billy Ray but found himself leaning against a small hand planted firm against his chest. Vern stood a head and a half taller than Denise, but he stopped short like she was overpowering him.

"Will you please quit embarrassing me?" Denise pleaded.

Vern blinked. "Embarrassing you? Honey, you know I wouldn't ever want to do anything to embarrass you."

"Well you *are*," she snapped.

"But . . ."

She turned and fixed Billy Ray with a look that put him in his place too. "And you. You're a preacher. You should know better. Haven't you been listening to all the things you've been teaching me? Don't you believe all the nice things you've said?"

"Teaching you?" Vern yelped. "Since

when has this pipsqueak preacher been teaching you stuff, Denise?"

"I'll turn the other cheek," Billy Ray said. "*Then* I'll whip him."

"Who the hell d'you think you'll whip?" Vern snarled.

"Both of you hush. Nobody is going to whip anybody. I swear, one of you is as bad as the other."

She gave Vern a push, shoving him back toward his horse, in spite of the disparity between her slight bulk and his.

"There isn't going to be anymore of this," Denise said. "Not today and not any other day either."

She glared at Vern, and under the harsh light of Denise's disapproval he reluctantly took his reins back and swung onto the saddle. Derek Trumaine brought his horse forward through the crowd until he was beside Vern.

Denise waited until Vern was firmly seated, then she turned and marched over to Billy Ray. She yanked at his elbow to turn him so he stood meekly beside her, facing Vern and the pack of cowboys.

"For your information," she told them, "I am going to be joining this church congregation myself. And I don't want to see any of you around here again unless it's to come to services with us."

"Denise!" Vern protested loudly.

"I mean it, Daddy. I want you to lay off too. If these farmers can't make it, that's their problem and Billy Ray's, but I won't have any of you or the hands being a part of it. Or you either, Derek. You all leave them be."

What had she just called Vern? Billy Ray thought. He must not have heard it right.

Denise turned, eyes flashing until he expected to see smoke curling out of her ears. She looked him square in the face. "And you," she accused. "You give all this good advice and then you run away so I can't take it. How come you haven't been showing up at the riverbank all this week? Well?"

This time it was Billy Ray who was gaping and gasping for air.

"You told me to declare myself, Billy Ray Halstad. Well all right. Right here in front of God and all these people, I'm declaring it."

"Declaring what?"

Her nerve faltered. Her eyes dropped away from his. "You know what," she said in a small voice.

Billy Ray felt his heart lift and soar toward the heavens.

He threw his head back and roared with joy.

He grabbed Denise in a hug, right there in front of God and all those people, in front of the farmers and the cowboys both.

"Thanks. Hey, Boss. You hear me? Thank You," he shouted.

"Denise. Honey."

"Go home, Papa. Take the hands and go home. Please?" She quite deliberately slipped closer inside Billy Ray's arm. Right there for everybody to see. "So. *Now* do you think I'm a hussy?" she demanded in a mutter that was intended for Billy Ray's ear only.

He grinned at her. "We'll discuss it. Later. In private." He added a wink to that promise. Hey, he'd told Emmy, hadn't he, that kissing wasn't a sin. Not if the intentions were honorable. Well, maybe it *was* time he started listening to himself when he gave advice.

"Go home, Papa."

Most of the cowboys were already turning away. Derek leaned over and whispered something to his father, and Vern Trumaine reluctantly reined his mount back toward town.

Denise giggled and fitted herself closer against Billy Ray. "You'll love them once you get to know them. Really."

Billy Ray made a face.

261

It was just now occurring to him that Vern and Derek Trumaine were going to be his in-laws. And just as soon as he could decently make that so.

He glanced upward. "Just couldn't let it go without pulling a prank on me, could You?"

He felt Denise moving slightly away from him. She was smiling and nodding and speaking.

As the cowboys moved away, the farmers and their families were moving in closer.

There were introductions to be made, and welcomes to be said and a dinner to be eaten.

Denise acted like she was part of it already.

Billy Ray felt his chest puff with pride as Denise made herself known to all the folks of Purgatory City's church congregation.

If he didn't quit this grinning pretty soon his jaw was going to go into cramps. But he just couldn't make himself stop.

"Thanks," he whispered again, as he stepped in behind Denise and went to shaking hands with the good folks who were his flock.

About the Author

Billy Ray's Forty Days is the tenth Double D Western by **Frank Roderus**. Some of the others include *Charlie and the Sir*, *Finding Nevada*, *Stillwater Smith*, and *Leaving Kansas*, which won the Western Writers of America's Spur Award for Best Western Novel in 1983.

He lives in Florida.

The employees of Thorndike Press hope you have enjoyed this Large Print book. All our Thorndike and Wheeler Large Print titles are designed for easy reading, and all our books are made to last. Other Thorndike Press Large Print books are available at your library, through selected bookstores, or directly from us.

For information about titles, please call:

(800) 223-1244

or visit our Web site at:

www.gale.com/thorndike
www.gale.com/wheeler

To share your comments, please write:

Publisher
Thorndike Press
295 Kennedy Memorial Drive
Waterville, ME 04901